THE VERY THOUGHT OF YOU
Pacific Vista Ranch, Book 2
Copyright © 2019 by Claire Marti

eBook 978-1-7333046-2-7
Print book 978-1-7333046-3-4



This is a work of fiction. Names, characters, places and incidents are either the product of the author's imagination or are used fictitiously, and any resemblance to actual persons, living or dead, business establishments, events or locales is entirely coincidental.

Printed in the USA.

Cover Design and Interior Format

# The Very Thought Of You

PACIFIC VISTA RANCH

BOOK TWO

## CLAIRE MARTI

# DEDICATION

*To Todd…for everything.*

# ACKNOWLEDGEMENTS

WRITING A BOOK IS DEFINITELY a team effort and I have to admit Amanda and Jake's story required a huge team. I'm so grateful for all the support I received.

Big thanks to Tim Fodrey, Fire Captain in Carlsbad, California, for all the detailed information on the path to become a fire captain. Thank you for all you do. Big thanks to my veterinarian Yolanda Plute Kenney, D.V.M., for sharing her knowledge on treating dogs and horses. I appreciate all the details of being an equine veterinarian I learned from Lea Ann Baucom, D.V.M. Once again, thank you Kasey Bennett, Farm Manager of Ocean Breeze Ranch, for your input and knowledge about all things horse-related.

To Dylan Jones——thank you for all your wise input on learning processing issues and being the best listener on all topics. Thanks to everyone who read early versions, offered input at various stages, listened to me moan and groan, and offered your invaluable assistance: Kay Bennett, Joanna Kelly, Megan Randall, Michele Arris, Kerrigan Byrne, and Lacy Pope——you each help me more than you could imagine. I appreciate your time and opinions.

To my wonderful editor, Lindsey Faber, thank you for helping me polish this story from start to finish. To my brother Robert Petretti—thanks for your love and support, both as my big brother and as proofreader extraordinaire.

Last but not least, to Todd for waiting patiently while I wrote into the wee hours. I love you. And, finally to my furry kids: Lola, Beau and Josie, thanks for providing me unconditional love.

# CHAPTER 1

JAKE CRUZ GRIMACED DOWN AT the books and laptop computer stacked on the passenger seat of his pick-up. What the hell had he gotten himself into now? Becoming a fire captain with the Rancho Santa Fe Fire Department was for people with book smarts, not guys like him. Although he had almost a decade of experience under his firefighting belt, he didn't stand a chance at a promotion without a Bachelor's in Emergency Management.

He and school didn't mix.

Without tutors, he would never have graduated high school. He'd nursed a crush on the beautiful senior girl who'd helped him pass freshman Algebra, although she'd only seen him as another student. She'd been compassionate and kind and hadn't treated him like he was stupid. Unlike almost everybody else in school. His other tutors had helped him, but he'd never felt the same sense of acceptance like he had from Amanda McNeill.

Wow, the prospect of cracking those books open was sure stirring up the past. He slapped his palm on the steering wheel. He'd managed to become a firefighter and pass all the tests along the way without anybody's help, although he'd probably taken twice as long to study as the other candidates. And god knew he'd probably be an old man by the time he finished his online degree. But he would conquer this challenge if it were the last thing he did.

A loud thump jolted his attention back where it should be––on the road. The shiny Mercedes in front of him raced off in a squeal of tires. Jake cursed when he saw a brown animal splayed out in the middle of the lane and swerved to the narrow shoulder. What kind of person hit an animal and kept going?

Luckily, nobody was behind him. He leapt out of the truck and ran to the middle of the street where a medium-sized dog lay in a rapidly expanding scarlet pool. *Damn it.* Although he usually employed his crisis training for humans, he'd rescued enough animals from fires to be confident the same rules applied.

One chocolate brown eye gazed up at him, and a bright pink tongue lolled out of the animal's mouth. Harsh pants filled the air. At least she was breathing, even if she was hyperventilating. He crouched down and laid one palm on the dog's neck to comfort her.

"It's okay, girl, I'm here. I'll help you." The car had been speeding, at least away from the scene, and clipped the poor dog hard. Jerks. From a quick visual, it didn't appear anything was broken, but too much vivid red blood poured from numerous lacerations. She needed treatment and she needed it ASAP.

Jake looked around, getting his bearings. He knew these winding tree-lined roads of Rancho Santa Fe so well he could navigate them blindfolded. Of course, none of the local veterinarians were nearby. Damn it, it would be a good twenty minutes before he could reach an animal hospital. Twenty minutes could be too long. He pinched the bridge of his nose and closed his eyes for a moment.

His eyes flew open. Pacific Vista Ranch, a large quarter-horse breeding ranch run by the McNeill family, was about a mile away. Coincidentally, the very same Amanda McNeill he'd been reminiscing about was the resident equine veterinarian. Even if Amanda worked almost exclusively with horses, she could still help a dog, right?

He scooped up the collarless dog and carried her to his truck. Fortunately, he had a blanket on the back seat. He gingerly tucked the edges of the fleece around her. The pup whimpered at the contact, but watched him with trusting eyes.

"It's going to be okay, girl, I promise. Just hold tight." He used the soothing tone he'd mastered from years of emergency medical house calls.

Once she was secure on the back seat, he hopped into the driver's seat and steered his truck back onto the road. Amanda would help the sweet pup, wouldn't she?

His fingers tightened around the steering wheel and he drew in a deep breath. Ready or not, he was going to see Amanda again for the second time since ninth grade. Unlike last summer when he'd been out at the McNeills' sprawling ranch because of a local fire, he couldn't pretend like he didn't know her. He'd been struck dumb by her beauty when he'd stepped off the fire truck. His teenage crush hadn't recognized him. Nobody from high school did.

But now wasn't the time to contemplate. The injured dog was his first priority. Jake exhaled, pulled up to the guard's station beside an enormous wooden and stone gate, and rolled down his window.

A dark-haired guy in a crisp white shirt glanced up at him and grabbed a clipboard. "Hello. What's your name and who are you here to see?" It figured the McNeills had a list of approved visitors.

"Jake Cruz. I'm a local fireman. Here to see Dr. McNeill. It's an emergency." He swallowed, his throat suddenly dry.

"An emergency? A fire?" The guard's black brows lifted over mirrored sunglasses.

"No, not a fire. Some jerk hit a dog and kept driving. I've got her on the back seat and she's losing a lot of blood. She's got to see a vet fast."

The guard peered into the back of the truck. "Oh man, what's wrong with people? I'm sure Dr. McNeill will want to help. I'll buzz you in and call up to the office to let her know you're here. The vet buildings are beyond the house and before the stables."

"Yeah, I'll find them. Thanks." Jake hit the gas

and cruised through the open gates.

Flashes of lush trees, rolling hills, and bright flowers shrouded the curving road, but he didn't have time to admire the scenery. What were the odds he'd actually been thinking about Amanda and now he was arriving on her doorstep, asking for help?

When he pulled into the parking area in front of a single-story brick building, the double glass doors flew open. Dr. Amanda McNeill ran toward him in a rush of golden hair and mile-long legs. His breath lodged in his throat and his mind blanked. Holy hell—she was stunning.

"Scott said you've got a dog that was hit by a car? Where?" Her voice was as cool and smooth as his favorite premium tequila.

Before he could reply, she was peering over his shoulder through the truck's driver-side window. Hints of a fresh beachy scent wafted toward him when her long, silky hair brushed against him. He remained rooted to his seat, his tongue heavy as a brick in his mouth. Just as tongue-tied as he'd been around her in high school.

So much for his EMT and Paramedic training and swift reflexes. Apparently, they'd vanished. He shook his head, willing his brain to function.

"She's in the back. I'll carry her in." His motor coordination returned and he stepped out of the car, careful not to touch her and lose the remainder of his usually razor-sharp instincts.

Amanda stepped back and Jake gently picked up the dog, wrapping the edges of the blanket around her matted fur. She remained motionless and silent, gazing up at him.

"Well, she's lucky you were there. Come on, let's get her inside." Amanda turned and hurried toward the entrance.

Walking behind her, he couldn't help but notice her graceful stride and the hint of a slender form beneath her white doctor's coat. Hell, he remembered those long, willowy limbs from over a decade ago. The dog whimpered and Jake murmured reassuring words to her.

"Place her on the table, please." Jake followed Amanda into a pristine treatment room and placed the dog onto a shiny metal examination table. He grimaced when she raised pleading brown eyes toward him. Nobody liked going to the doctor.

"Can you save her?"

Amanda unwrapped the blanket covering the injured dog. Her eyebrows drew together when the material stuck to the bloody wounds. "Well, I haven't treated a dog since vet school, but I do treat the barn cats when they let me, so I'll do my best."

She stroked the animal's head and smiled down at her. "It's going to be okay, girl."

She checked the mutt's breathing, listening to her heart and lungs. The dog lay motionless and kept her gaze locked on Amanda.

"Her breathing is shallow and fast, but that's probably from the scare. I don't think she needs an x-ray at this point, which is good because I'd need to take her down to the small animal vet in town."

Jake's shoulders relaxed.

She lifted up the dog's lip. "Okay, her gums are pink, so although it looks like she's lost a lot of skin and blood, she's not in shock. Hopefully, once I clean her up, her injuries won't be too severe. Dogs are tougher than we give them credit for."

Amanda gently continued the exam. When her hand reached the dog's rear flank, the animal whimpered. "Oh sweetheart, I'm so sorry. Her rear leg definitely took the brunt of the impact. She's got terrible road rash."

"Do you think her leg's broken?"

Amanda frowned. "I don't think so. I need to flush out the wounds and give her some pain meds and an antibiotic. I just need to calculate how much of the equine painkiller will work for her so I don't give her too much. Luckily, I've got some cat antibiotics, which should work." Amanda raised her gaze to his.

Her eyes were the clearest jade green he'd ever seen, like the lush meadows of her family's ranch. Not a hint of blue or gray or yellow. He swallowed and tried to find his voice. "Um…can I help? I'm off for the rest of the afternoon."

She shook her head. "My assistant is on his way up. Why, do you have medical training?"

He nodded. "Yeah, I'm a firefighter paramedic."

Recognition dawned in her eyes and her brows drew together over her small straight nose. "Firefighter? Did you come out during the fire last summer? You look familiar."

"Yeah."

She reached one narrow strong hand out to him. "I'm sorry, I ran out so quickly when Scott called, I didn't introduce myself. I'm Amanda McNeill."

*Shit. Should he admit he knew exactly who she was?* His hand shot out before he opened his mouth. A shot of awareness speared up his arm at the firm pressure of her cool smooth skin against his. "Jake Cruz."

"Well, Jake, I think she's going to be just fine, thanks to you saving her and bringing her here so quickly. I should be able to take it from here. Are you planning on keeping her?"

"Keeping her?"

"Well, she doesn't have a collar and the pads of her feet are worn down, so I suspect she was abandoned or maybe she escaped and has been wandering for a while. You're her hero." She smiled at him, her huge emerald eyes crinkling at the corners.

Did *she* see him as a hero? Jake's breath bottled up in his chest and he looked down at the dog. It was safer than staring into Amanda's heart-shaped face.

"Not sure I'm a hero. I work hectic hours, so I may not be the right home for her, but I could ask around..." He trailed off and forced himself to meet her gaze. *And I want to see you again.* "Can you let me know how she's doing?"

"Sure. Give me your number and I'll update you." The corners of her full, pink lips curved up.

Every muscle in his body stiffened. Visions of

Amanda McNeill had colored his daydreams for years. Hell, he'd dreamt about her at night too. Being in her presence now was messing with his equilibrium. How could the reality of this woman blow away the fantasy of the kind, intelligent girl from high school?

A stocky young guy hurried through the door, pushing a padded cart. "What do you need, Dr. McNeill?"

"Russ, can you please bring her back and draw up a mini dose of Banamine or Butorphanol—whichever is more convenient—to clean out all her abrasions? We need to flush out the gravel and asphalt and debris. I'll be there in five."

"On it. Poor girl." The assistant transferred the animal onto the cart and wheeled her out of the room.

"You'll see her again, don't worry." Amanda's eyes glinted with warmth when she looked back at Jake. "I'll walk you out."

He nodded. Was she being nice because she was a nice person or could she also feel the electricity sparking between them? He squared his shoulders and put one foot in front of the other. He'd act cool, not like the nerdy teenager he'd been.

"Just give me your number and I'll text you after I've finished cleaning her up." She fished a cell phone out of the pocket of her pristine white coat when they reached his truck.

He shared his number, but didn't imagine anything at all as he watched her long slender fingers punch them into her phone. Nope, no visions of her raking those short, unpainted fingernails down his back. Sweat broke out between his shoulder blades.

Okay, he needed to get out of here before he said something stupid or pounced on her. He opened his truck door and wished he were a smooth talker like his big brother. Wished he had a clever exit line.

She dropped the phone back into her pocket and looked up. Her eyes narrowed on the pile of books on his passenger seat and she tilted her head. "Are you in school?"

He nodded. Suddenly he was sweating for real. She would connect the dots.

"Wait a second. You said your name was Jake Cruz?" Her gaze swept from the top of his head all the way down his 6'5 frame and back up again. "You aren't…? Did you go to Torrey Pines?"

Busted. Why the hell hadn't he said so earlier? "Yeah, I am and I did. You were my math tutor when I was a freshman and you were a senior."

Her eyes grew enormous. "But you were…"

"A scrawny little hundred pounder. Yeah, I hit a growth spurt after you graduated." Jake shrugged but heat flooded his cheeks, belying what he hoped was a nonchalant response.

She cleared her throat, "Um, I'd say so. Why didn't you remind me before?"

He bit the inside of his cheek and stared down at his size 14 running shoes. "I dunno, not sure you'd remember me."

"I remember everyone I tutored, but I didn't

recognize you, you're so huge." A pink hue flushed her high cheekbones. "I'm sorry, that came out wrong."

He laughed and his shoulders relaxed. Maybe she was nervous around him too. "Yeah, I grew about a foot in tenth grade and now I've got to stay strong for my job. Working out was always easier for me than studying."

She gestured toward the books on his seat. "So what's with the textbooks?"

"Well, I got my diploma, but to move up in the fire department it's really helpful to have a Bachelor's, so I just started an online program." *Which I'm terrified I'll fail.*

"I think that's great. How's it going?" She smiled.

"I've got my first test this week, so we'll see." Yeah, he'd have to wait to get into his truck because the back of his shirt was drenched with sweat. Not nervous around her at all. Nor was he stressed about that test. Denial was obviously a sweaty endeavor.

"You've got this. I've got to see to the dog, but I'll text you soon." She brushed his forearm and her feather-light touch shot sparks of heat straight from his arm to his groin.

"Thanks." Hell, had he grunted his response? He wasn't a talkative guy to begin with, but around her, he sounded like a caveman.

She turned and sauntered back to her clinic. Frozen to the spot, he watched every single step. Once the door closed behind her, he climbed into his truck and stared out the windshield without flicking on the ignition. For years, he'd imagined seeing her again as a man and not an insecure little boy.

Would she live up to the pedestal he'd placed her upon? He'd compared every woman he'd met to his memory of her as the ideal woman. Every single one failed to hold a candle to Amanda McNeill.

Now he'd actually seen her and spoken with her? He hadn't exaggerated her positive qualities nor minimized her flaws. She was more kind than he remembered. More beautiful. More everything.

So what was he going to do about it?

# CHAPTER 2

AFTER DOUBLE-CHECKING TO MAKE SURE the sweet fifty-pound mutt she'd named Stella was settled, Amanda returned to her office. She sank into the comfy swivel chair in front of her perfectly organized teak desk. Closing her eyes, she leaned her head back and allowed herself to relax. An image of broad shoulders, sculpted chest, and sinewy forearms sprinkled with dark hair flashed into her mind. She shivered, recalling how warm and smooth his bronze skin had been when she'd touched him. Sparks had crackled off him, singeing her fingertips.

And then his face: intense obsidian eyes surrounded with a dense thicket of eyelashes, a strong nose that looked like it had been broken a time or three, hollow cheeks, and a jaw hewn from granite. Would he appear less forbidding if his solemn expression were replaced with a grin or laughter?

He resembled one of the actors from the *Magic Mike* movies her sisters had forced her to watch. Or a guy from one of those charity calendars where impossibly gorgeous firefighters posed with puppies or kittens. How in the world was he the sweet, skinny kid she'd tutored?

Back in high school, he'd rarely met her gaze when they had worked together to cope with his processing issues. But when he didn't think she would notice, she'd often caught him staring at her with big, adoring eyes. At that point, her life had just been upended after her mom died and her family had been forced to leave L.A., so his innocent crush had been a sweet respite during a tough time. He'd even brought her a bouquet of flowers at the end of the school year after he'd passed his finals. His cheeks had been beet red and he couldn't meet her gaze when he'd mumbled a thank you.

Sweet. And innocent.

Like a little brother.

Now, while it was sweet he'd saved the dog, there was nothing innocent about him. On the contrary, he'd had a dangerous glint in his dark eyes when he'd described the car that had hit Stella and sped off. And a man that ripped, powerful, and huge couldn't be innocent. More like dangerously sexy.

And who was the one with a crush now? A not so innocent crush. She'd been unable to read his reaction, which wasn't surprising because her flirting skills could be categorized as rusty, at best. Another tingle shot down her spine as she imagined Jake kissing her with that tempting mouth. Her cheeks flamed remembering how she'd blurted out the comment about him being huge.

Enough. She opened her eyes and straightened

her spine. Back to the reality of managing quarter-horse breeding season while her younger sister, the ranch manager, was out of town. Sam was on a short mini-honeymoon with her husband Holt. Amanda had insisted she would keep everything under control and her time was planned in fifteen-minute increments. After the few hours she'd taken to help Stella, she was behind schedule.

Because she was the reliable, sensible McNeill sister, she always fulfilled her promises. And she'd promised to text Jake. Her meandering thoughts about how he might look without that fitted black t-shirt wouldn't translate via text, right?

She grabbed her phone, took a cleansing breath, and typed. *Hi Jake, everything went great and Stella's going to be fine.*

Her screen remained blank so she set the phone down and turned to her computer to tackle the seemingly endless stream of paperwork. A flash of light caught her eye. Text incoming. She snatched up the phone.

*Stella? Perfect name. What's next?*

Amanda leaned back into her cushy leather chair and tapped one finger against her lips. Good question.

*I'll keep her here while she heals & make sure nobody has reported her lost. What do you think about fostering her?*

From what she knew, the firefighters in Rancho Santa Fe worked twenty-four hour shifts and could often be at the station for days at a time. Not really ideal to have a pet, but didn't you always see pictures of dogs and firemen? Or was she confusing Jake with those hot fireman calendars again? Jake Cruz could be on the cover of one of those.

*Maybe we could both foster her?*

Amanda frowned. After Kola, her family's lab mix, died a few years ago, they hadn't adopted a new dog. A dog meant permanence. And responsibility.

Granted, her dad and stepmom lived in one wing of their sprawling home, her younger sister Dylan lived in another wing with her, and Sam and Holt lived in one of the guest houses. They'd all most likely be happy to help out. If she committed to fostering Stella, she'd be obligated to stay close. And for the first time in her adult life, she'd grown weary of being the dependable sister.

Last summer, the McNeills' private lifestyle ended when her dad allowed a movie to be filmed at the ranch and the press resurrected the tragic decade-old story surrounding her mom's death. Articles about how Chris McNeill abandoned his Hollywood Producer/Director career and moved his three daughters to exclusive Rancho Santa Fe to escape the ugly rumors and relentless paparazzi harassment were once again front-page news. After a dozen years of a secluded life, everything shifted.

Unfamiliar sensations of restlessness and isolation plagued her for the first time. The rest of her family seemed to be exploring new paths. Her dad was once again behind the camera, back in Hollywood part-time. After escaping to Paris last summer, Dylan's dedication to launching her art career had deepened. And she'd never seen new-lywed Sam so blissful.

Shouldn't she be seizing the day or something too? Yeah, right. Sensible, predictable Amanda excelled at work, read books, rode horses, and rarely dated. Being borderline boring never both-ered her before, but now she'd started questioning everything.

For goodness sake, she was only thirty years old and was already a fixture on her family's ranch. Ever since she'd returned to California when she was twenty-four, she'd been Pacific Vista Ranch's resident equine vet. She'd even lived on the ranch during college, graduating from University of California at San Diego in three years and grad-uating magna cum laude from Virginia Tech Veterinary School. And here she was: goody-goody Amanda McNeill.

Maybe she needed to take a sabbatical and travel the world or…something. She snorted.

*Share her? How do you mean?*

Jake's answer popped up. *I could keep her on my 4 days off between shifts & drop her off on way to station.*

Amanda's heart warmed at his refreshing offer to share responsibility for Stella. Who knew what could happen if they saw each other weekly? Jake Cruz's appearance on her doorstep could be the beginning of something new. Her pulse acceler-ated.

*That could work.* And would be an excuse to see if she'd imagined the chemistry between them.

*When can I visit?*

A distinct tingling in her belly joined her quickened pulse. She couldn't remember the last time she'd experienced these physical sensations with a guy. *Why don't you give her a couple days to recover more? Maybe Thursday?*

His reply flashed immediately. *2 on Thursday?*

She smiled. The rest of her family would be out of town until the weekend. Dylan usually spent most of the day holed up in her studio painting. Without everyone breathing down her neck, she'd have a chance to analyze the arrangement.

*Sure. I'll be here.* She snorted again—she was always at the ranch. Like one of the stables or the vet buildings.

*See you then.*

She texted a thumbs-up and placed the phone down. Her lips curved up and she allowed her eyes to flutter closed for just one more minute before she returned to work.

"Hold still, I've got to paint that expression. I'll call it *Bliss*." Her younger sister Dylan's voice chirped. "What gives with the Cheshire cat grin?"

Amanda jolted upright. "You almost gave me a heart attack, sneaking up on me like that."

"I didn't sneak. I walked in like I usually do; you were just off in la-la land. C'mon, I've had a frustratingly uninspired day. Tell me." Dylan perched on the edge of the desk and flashed her gorgeous grin.

"Well, you've got some blue paint on your face—did you miss the canvas?" Amanda laughed.

"I do have some news."

"Yeah? Anything exciting?" Dylan's big brown eyes widened and she rubbed at her face.

"Well, I think I've got a foster dog." Amanda summarized the dog's rescue.

Dylan's slender artist's hands curled into fists. "There's a special ring of hell for people who hurt animals. So, who is this Jake the dog-saver?"

Heat rose in Amanda's cheeks and she prayed her sister didn't notice. "He was just behind the car that hit Stella."

Dylan's eyes widened. "Why are we fostering her? Did you speak to her owners?"

Amanda shook her head. "I think she was dumped or abandoned. I named her Stella. So, Jake and I agreed to share custody—"

"Together?" Dylan brows flew up and she hopped off the edge of the desk.

"Do you want to hear it or not?" Amanda fell back on her usual serene tone, which always worked to quiet her family.

Dylan covered her mouth with one hand and gestured with the other for her to continue. Amanda quickly explained the proposed arrangement.

Her sister narrowed her eyes. "Okay. That makes sense, but you're hiding something. What does Mr. Jake Cruz, Fireman, look like?"

Amanda bit the inside of her lower lip. "What he looks like has nothing to do with it. I mean, we haven't had a dog since Kola and I'd love the company." *Liar liar, pants on fire.*

"The dog's company or the company of what I suspect to be a very hot fireman. Does he look like that guy in *Magic Mike*?"

Amanda's mouth fell open. "How did you know that?"

Dylan laughed and squeezed Amanda's hands. "Oh my god, seriously? No way he looks like that guy. Does he?"

Amanda nodded and fanned her cheeks with one hand. "He is like six foot five, dark, and brooding. But…"

"And? What? I haven't seen you this animated talking about a guy since…" Dylan smirked. "About never?"

Amanda cleared her throat. "So, he does look like that actor, but that's not the surprising part. It turns out he was actually one of the students I tutored back in high school, but I didn't recognize him."

"Didn't recognize him?"

Amanda nodded. "No. In high school, he was about five foot six and one hundred pounds and now his muscles have muscles. And wow."

"I thought the hunky firefighters usually saved cats? Something new? How old is he?"

Amanda considered. "Around your age. Twenty-seven or twenty-eight? What's kind of sweet is he didn't admit to knowing me right away. I think he might have been embarrassed I didn't remember him."

"Ooh, the scrawny freshman with a crush on his senior tutor. It's like a 1980s romcom. Are you playing the cougar? Maybe it's fate." Dylan laughed and clapped her hands together.

Amanda snorted. "Three years do not a cougar make. I don't know about the romcom idea. But…" She gazed out the window at the bright blue sky.

"But he's a gorgeous dog-saving hunk who crushed on you in high school. Sounds meant to be. You've seemed restless lately, why not go out with him?"

"Go out with him?"

"Um, yes. Like a date. You know, two people go and have food, drink, and possibly enjoy other activities together? How long has it been since you've been on a date anyway?" Dylan asked.

"Forever." She sighed. Time to change the subject.

Dylan wagged a finger at her. "That sounds right. You need to have more fun."

Amanda sighed. "It's tough to meet guys because I'd rather read a book than go online or go out and make small talk at a bar."

"You sound like you're ninety. I think one thing we've all realized since last summer is that we've been pretty secluded. Spending a few months in Paris sure opened my eyes." Dylan's thick dark brows drew together.

"Nothing feels the same anymore, does it?"

"Nope. But you're still the resident equine vet who stays home too much and I'm still the moody artist who goes out too much." The corner of Dylan's full lips hitched up.

Amanda reached for her sister's hands and squeezed. "You don't go out too much."

"Don't change the subject. We were talking about you." Dylan's dark eyes grew serious. "Are you attracted to this Jake guy?"

Amanda nodded. "Yeah, I actually am. But what if he just wants Stella?"

Dylan snorted and pulled Amanda up out of the chair. "I think he wants you, and Stella's the icing on the cake. Go for it. A gorgeous fireman is just the ticket to get you out of your rut."

"I am not in a rut." More like a Grand-Canyon-sized crater.

Dylan chuckled. "Yes you are. So, can I meet this little cupid?"

Amanda threaded her arm through her sister's and they headed back to the recovery room. "Cupid. You're a hoot. I'll keep an open mind about getting to know Jake better."

"Even just to see him without his shirt?" Dylan waggled her eyebrows.

"Or that." Her cheeks flamed again. Would she ever cool down visualizing his broad chest and washboard abs without his shirt?

# CHAPTER 3

JAKE TUCKED THE EDGES OF his favorite Rolling Stones vintage t-shirt into the waist of his new jeans. He double-checked his reflection in the truck's rearview mirror. He'd showered and shaved and didn't have spinach from his post-workout smoothie in his teeth. He figured Stella wouldn't care what he looked like, but he wanted to make a good impression on Amanda.

His pulse was hammering and he hadn't even seen Amanda yet. He forced himself to take some long steady breaths, just like he encouraged the patients he dealt with during emergency calls. Was he seriously panting at the idea of seeing her again? Would he drool too?

He softened his death grip on the door handle, willing himself to relax. Despite his efforts to shake his crappy mood with a punishing hundred burpees and a ten-mile run, he couldn't stop thinking about his first test. He hadn't received the grade yet, but he was pretty damn sure it wouldn't be an A. Or even a C. Although the online program was flexible and was giving him some allowances for his learning issues, they certainly wouldn't compromise if he couldn't pass the courses.

History repeating itself. Just like during school. He'd hidden his reading challenges from his parents as long as he could. The school required him to repeat second grade because they just thought he was a slow learner. A really slow learner.

Other kids had made fun of him and some had even bullied him. All he'd figured was he liked playing outside or doing anything but reading or homework. When his fifth grade teacher finally realized he couldn't pass a test to save his life, she'd stepped in. But the damage from his processing issues had already been done. He'd finished school and succeeded in his firefighting training, but every step was a battle.

He shook himself back to the present, whipped open the truck door, and strode to the vet clinic's entrance. His ninth grade crush was definitely still in place and he was optimistic about seeing Amanda. Today, he'd make sure she saw him as an equal instead of a little boy who sucked at math.

He entered the building and gazed around the empty, spacious lobby. Sunlight shining through enormous windows illuminated the pristine room. A long row of bench seating ran along the far wall, with bright plaid cushions and pillows inviting visitors to curl up in the sunshine. A long L-shaped counter created a barrier to the closed doors behind it. Where were Amanda and their dog?

Their dog? Yep, he was already thinking of

Stella that way.

One of the doors opened and Amanda emerged. She wasn't wearing a shapeless white coat today. Snug jeans emphasized her long legs and a yellow Blondie concert t-shirt highlighted her slender shape. Her blond hair was secured back into a high ponytail and holy hell––her slender neck was gorgeous––and totally kissable. He swallowed, his mouth parched.

"Hi Jake, you're right on time. Stella's been improving, so I figured we could take her for a short walk." She smiled, flashing even white teeth, and walked around the edge of the counter with the dog.

He managed to keep his jaw from falling open. She was the most beautiful woman he'd ever seen. *Focus on the dog, dude.*

"There's the beauty. She looks great." He crossed the room and crouched down. No longer bloody and traumatized, Stella was fluffy, shiny, and grinning at him. Her tail began thumping and she leaned in to slather his face with kisses. He laughed and scratched behind her floppy ears.

"So turns out once we washed her, she's more butterscotch than brown. And I forgot to warn you, she's the kissing bandit." Amanda said.

"What do you think she is?" If he stared at Amanda's full pink lips, *he'd* be the kissing bandit. He focused on the dog.

"I'm not sure, but I think she's part lab with either some boxer or shepherd. Her white socks and chest sure look like boxer markings, but her head is all lab." She stroked Stella's head.

Amanda's hands were gorgeous, just like the rest of her. Maybe he was going to drool after all. *Focus on the dog. Do not think about those hands.*

"Yeah, I see the boxer too. Well, she looks like she's going to be fine. Will her fur grow back?" He examined her right side and flank, which were still angry red and missing patches of fur.

"Come on, let's walk her and I'll fill you in." She handed him the hot pink leash and their fingers brushed. She snatched her hand away and stepped back.

"After you." Maybe she felt the sparks too. He smiled to himself. "Let's head over toward the stables so I can see how Stella reacts to the horses." She skirted around him, with no apparent reaction to the electricity crackling in the air around them.

No way was the chemistry his imagination. From his observation, they were alike, calm and in control on the surface. In his years dealing with emergencies, he had to act stoic, even if he was freaking out inside. He'd perfected an unruffled exterior and a few girls he'd dated had even accused him of having ice water running through his veins. What was she really feeling beneath her serene façade? Amanda's worn cowboy boots crunched along the gravel path and her ponytail swayed as she walked. The dog trotted along like nothing had ever happened, pausing to sniff a rose bush and nibble on some long blades of grass. It was as if she'd lived on the ranch forever and this was just one of her routine strolls.

"That car was flying, but Stella seems to be walking fine." Jake said.

Amanda angled her head toward him. "Right? Animals are really resilient. Stella was lucky."

"Yeah. Any word from the shelters or vets?" Walking with Amanda and Stella could become a habit.

"Nobody has claimed her yet." She frowned. "So, did you become a fireman right out of school?"

He nodded. "Well, I started training right after I graduated high school. I became an EMT, then a paramedic, and then finally was able to apply to be one."

"Did you always want to be a fireman?"

"My uncle who lives in Colorado was a fire captain and my hero." The tight muscles on the back of his neck relaxed.

"That's great." Her pink lips curved up. "I knew I wanted to be a vet when I was ten years old. It's kind of cool to have that certainty as a kid, right?"

He nodded. Okay, now they shared at least three things in common, if you counted the dog and good taste in concert-t-shirts. "Yeah. It sure helped during some of the tougher times in train-ing."

"I've heard paramedic school is rough." She shook her head. "It takes a certain type of strength to constantly handle emergencies. I've got it easy here."

"Easy? Isn't veterinary school harder to get into

than medical school?" She was an Einstein-level genius, so maybe everything seemed easy.

She shrugged. "It was tough, but that was school. Now, I've got my routine with the horses during breeding season which usually isn't fraught with emergencies." Amanda's voice was crisp and quiet.

They crossed over rolling green hills in companionable silence. When he'd visited the ranch on prior fire business, he hadn't had the luxury of appreciating the natural beauty, but now he admired the lush landscape. Technicolor bursts of red, pink, and yellow flowers, along with every kind of tree imaginable lent the air a sweet fragrance. Jake drank it all in. Damn, this place was Nirvana.

Amanda stopped in front of an enormous barn. "So, we keep our personal horses and our stallion, Hercules, in the small stable. My mare, Bianca, is here."

"Small stable?" He managed not to let his mouth fall open.

She laughed, a musical sound. "Sorry, we've got four thirty-stall stables for the breeding operation. This one only has twenty-one."

The building was quiet, except for a few whinnies from the horses. Stella perked up and began sniffing the fresh air in earnest. How had this dog been bleeding out on the road a few days ago? He reached down and scratched behind her soft, golden ears. She gazed up at him with smiling chocolate eyes.

A white horse poked her head out of one of the stalls and Amanda immediately stroked her forehead. "Hi, sweet Bianca."

The mare preened under Amanda's attention and Jake smiled, observing her obvious bond with her horse. How would it feel to have those long, slender hands stroking him——he stiffened. No, he needed to get to know her before weaving fantasies around those elegant fingers. He swallowed a snort, like he hadn't been fantasizing about her since he was fifteen.

Amanda was inches away from him, with her beachy scent and sexy body. Would she feel as sweet as she looked? Desperately trying to resist the urge to span her narrow waist in his hands and pull her back against him, he forced himself to gaze down at the dog.

Stoic. Quiet. Self-disciplined.

Three of his top qualities had deserted him, overpowered by her proximity. "Are you bringing your horse out?" There, that was a reasonable question, right?

"Not right now. Then she'd think we were riding. Stella seems fine here in the stables, so that's great." Amanda turned, her eyes widened and her pupils dilated, but she didn't step back from him. All he needed to do was lean down and he could capture her tempting pink mouth with his. Their gazes remained locked and her lips parted.

He shoved his hands into his pockets so he didn't reach for her. "How do you think fostering is going?"

Amanda laughed. "I know how it goes. We fall in love and that's the end of the discussion."

Fall in love? Jake's chest tightened and he retreated a step. He'd never been in love. Could someone so perfect like Amanda ever fall in love with someone like him?

Oh, she had to be talking about falling for Stella.

He forced a short laugh. "Yeah, that's how we ended up with my family dog. I found him too and that was the end of the story."

"So, you're a rescuer too. Makes sense with your job. You're a good guy, Jake." She placed one cool hand on his forearm.

His skin burned where her hand had brushed against him. Damn. "I just like animals, that's all."

On the walk back to the house, Jake struggled to act nonchalant. She did seem to genuinely like him and the way her eyes had dilated when she'd looked at him? He wasn't imagining the chemistry.

Still, it felt premature to ask her out on a date. He'd wait until the next time they got together with the dog. Somehow fate, in the form of Stella, had brought Amanda McNeill back into his life and he wouldn't screw it up by acting like an overeager teenager. Like when he'd brought her flowers in high school.

This time around he was a man, not a shy little boy.

# CHAPTER 4

AMANDA ENTERED THE BARN TO check on Cowgirl, a sweetheart of a chestnut with a white star and stripe on her forehead. Marco, one of the grooms, had mentioned she seemed off this morning. At twenty-seven years old, the horse had always been healthy and happy, with a gentle maternal demeanor with the foals. In fact, she was one of their best-tempered nanny mares.

The stable was quiet, with most of the horses out to pasture for the day. Amanda put a lead on Cowgirl and walked her out into the fresh, crisp air, to an open grassy area. Cowgirl whinnied and nuzzled against her hand, acting perfectly normal.

The skies were as blue as the Pacific this morning, with a few fluffy cotton clouds saving the sky from sheer perfection. Amanda sighed and raised her face to the sun, savoring the warmth caressing her skin. Something fluttered in her belly as a picture of Jake popped into her brain. Was the gorgeous California firefighter with nerves of steel, strength of character, and a true desire to help others as sweet as the boy?

On Thursday, she'd caught him watching her

with those burning dark eyes when he thought she wasn't paying attention, just like when he was a kid. She swallowed, her throat suddenly parched. He still seemed shy, but as a reserved person herself, she knew the shell could conceal a lot. If he wanted to jump her bones half as much as she wanted to tear off his shirt every time she saw him, maybe she should make the first move.

Joint custody of Stella wouldn't last forever and if Jake didn't ask her out soon, she might not see him again. Especially if her family pushed to make Stella an official McNeill.

Cowgirl's head bumped against her shoulder and jolted Amanda back to the present. Here she was crushing on Jake like a teenage girl and ignoring her injured mare.

Well, he certainly was worth crushing on. She had eyes and a pulse, didn't she?

She stopped in the clearing and dropped the lead because she knew her sweet docile Cowgirl wouldn't go anywhere, not if the chance for a belly rub was in the picture. The horse loved having her belly stroked–– heck, loved any and all attention. But first, Amanda needed to examine her to see if something were indeed wrong.

Amanda patted down Cowgirl's shoulders, sides, front legs, and checked her front hooves. She stroked her left hindquarters and Cowgirl swished her tail. Amanda glanced up at her, but the horse appeared relaxed. So far so good. She came around the front again and stroked Cowgirl's forehead and crooned comforting words to her.

Cowgirl tossed her mane.

Amanda finished up her examination on her horse's right side. She checked out Cowgirl's inner leg and her fingers ran across a rough patch, which made Amanda look closer. Sure enough, there was a small wound. Maybe the horse had somehow gotten caught up in a little fencing or even gone too far into some of the rougher bushes out on the pasture.

Amanda straightened and reached into her small pack she'd brought along for a syringe of saline. Flushing out the wound wasn't complicated, and hopefully, with some ointment, Cowgirl would be good as new. She began cleaning the wound.

Cowgirl stiffened and swished her tail again.

"Shh. It's okay, girl, I don't want you getting an infection. I'm almost done." If any of the younger horses had exhibited the same signs, Amanda would have backed off. But this was her mellow old girl.

She pulled the salve out of the pack and squeezed some onto her fingertips. With one palm on Cowgirl's flank, she reached her other hand around to smooth the ointment onto the injured area.

Cowgirl swished her tail vigorously and stomped her foot.

"Only a few more seconds, sweet girl. Hold on for me." Amanda hurried to finish. She reached in for one last stroke and then Cowgirl's leg flew out and cow-kicked her. Hard.

Suddenly she was sailing through the air, her

arms grasping for purchase. With a resounding thump, she slammed onto the firm earth. Her breath whooshed out, stars danced behind her eyelids, and for a moment, time stood still. She'd landed on her left side, with her shoulder and hip bearing the brunt of the impact. A searing pain shot from her shoulder joint down to her elbow and she groaned.

Damn it, she'd misjudged Cowgirl.

"Cowgirl. What'd you have to do that for?" She gazed up at the horse, which stood in the exact same spot, as if nothing had happened.

"Well, I guess you didn't like the ointment, but did you have to kick me, girl? I'm just going to sit here for a moment." Lie here was more accurate. She lay flat on her back and stared up at the sky, inanely noticing how one cloud resembled a fire-breathing dragon. Her shoulder was screaming, her head was pounding, and she cursed under her breath. If she had to guess, she'd dislocated it at best, broken it at worst. Great. How in the world could she do her job if she had a broken shoulder?

She couldn't.

Once her breath began to regulate, she cautiously sat up. The excruciating pain in her shoulder spiked and her vision blurred. She needed to get back to the house and get to the doctor. Damn it. She didn't have time for this. Of course, all the grooms were down at the breeding barn, where she should be heading soon. Nobody was around.

And she hadn't brought her phone with her so

she couldn't call anybody. Self-sufficient was her middle name, but not so much right now. Today, her perfectionistic streak hadn't served her well. Why couldn't she have simply waited until Cowgirl relaxed? Because god forbid she leave any task undone. Now she was also having full conversations with herself. Nobody seeing her now would assume she was fine, like they usually did.

Because her vision wasn't clearing, she lay back down, holding her throbbing left elbow in her hand. She'd just lie here until she could figure out how she'd manage to return Cowgirl to her stall and walk back to the house. She squeezed her eyes shut and forced herself to slow down her breathing—hyperventilating wasn't going to solve anything.

Just a few more minutes and she'd get up.

"Amanda, are you okay?" A deep voice spoke from somewhere above her.

Her eyes flew open. Jake crouched down next to her, his brow furrowed. She shifted her gaze and Stella was staring down at her too, her head cocked to the side, mimicking Jake's expression somehow. Was she dreaming?

"Amanda, can you talk?" Jake's voice grew urgent.

"I've been better." Her voice cracked on the words and she bit her lip to avoid bursting into tears. "Cowgirl kicked me."

Jake looked up at the mare grazing on the grass nearby. "And you landed over here? Did you land on your back? Let me check to see if anything's broken."

"I landed on my left side. Shoulder's killing me." She pressed her lips together.

She winced when he gently stroked his large efficient hands expertly across her collarbones and shoulders, down her arms to her wrists. "My shoulder. Ouch."

"Let me help you sit up. Lean against me." His tone was calm and commanding.

She groaned and allowed him to help her to a seated position. Vaguely she was aware of the heat of his solid chest supporting her, but the stabbing and shooting pain racking her body sort of killed the passion. After a few moments of slow deep breathing, he helped her to her feet. Black dots swam before her eyes and if he hadn't been holding her up, she would have crumpled to the ground. Damn it.

She leaned against Jake's rock-hard body, grateful for the support. "I just need a couple minutes, but I'm okay. I think my shoulder is dislocated. We need to take Cowgirl back to the barn."

"Let me carry you, you're in pain," he rasped.

"I can walk. Can you get Cowgirl's lead?" Her knees buckled.

"I'm more worried about you than the horse." Before she could protest, he scooped her up in his arms, careful to cradle her right side against him. "I'm carrying you and I'll get her lead. Relax if you can." Jake grabbed Cowgirl's long lead and whistled for Stella to follow.

Relaxation wasn't in the cards anytime soon,

but despite the pain in her shoulder, heat pooled low in Amanda's belly. If she weren't in agony, she would have appreciated not just his efficiency, but the powerful arms and firm chest supporting her. Her eyelids floated shut. When he stopped walking, she forced herself to open them and look around.

They'd arrived at the barn. "Set me down for a moment and then just go put her in the third stall on the right. We'll let Marco know." The groom could check on Cowgirl.

Amanda's head was throbbing now, almost blinding her. Tears began streaming down her face. The pain in her shoulder was not just radiating down to her elbow, but up her neck and gripping the back of her skull like sharp forceps. She cradled her arm in her right hand and prayed for the twentieth time her shoulder wasn't broken. Her body was an aching, screaming mass of pain.

Jake swept her up again. "I'm taking you to the emergency room. Can someone watch Stella?" His long legs covered the ground to her house and he opened the door without releasing her from his arms.

"Dylan? Are you here?" She bellowed.

Jake didn't flinch, just shifted her in his arms, like she was light as a feather.

Dylan ran into the hallway, her long auburn hair flying behind her. "Amanda? Oh my god, are you okay? What happened?"

Amanda grimaced. She sucked in her breath as another flash of pain shot down her arm. "Long story short: Cowgirl cow-kicked me."

"I think her shoulder is dislocated and I need to get her to the ER pronto to make sure nothing's broken. Can you watch Stella?" Jake spoke up.

Dylan didn't hesitate. "Of course. Let me grab your purse and phone. I saw them on the counter. And you're Jake?"

"Dylan, this is Jake. Can we do formal introductions later? I'm dying." Amanda bit out the words.

Dylan hurried back from the kitchen and looped Amanda's purse over Jake's shoulder. "Call me as soon as you know anything, okay?"

"I'll make sure to text from her phone." Jake said and they were out the door.

"You've got a new habit of rescuing injured creatures these days." Amanda tried for a joke once he'd settled her into his truck's front seat.

"Shhh, just rest your head back and close your eyes. We'll be to the hospital soon." Jake sped to the Scripps Hospital Emergency Room in Encinitas, which seemed to take much longer than it should. Amanda worked to breathe slowly to manage the stabbing pain.

Jake parked and insisted on carrying her into the emergency room entrance. When she'd imagined him sweeping her off her feet, this scenario wasn't exactly what she'd pictured. At the moment, she couldn't truly appreciate being pressed against all those muscles. A young woman hurried toward them with a wheelchair.

"Hi Jake, are you on duty today?" The hospital aide furrowed her brows, but still managed to ogle him.

He placed Amanda in the wheelchair before responding. "Hi Karen, I'm not. My friend has a dislocated shoulder and possibly worse. Can you help us get her registered?"

She beamed at him. "Of course." She spared a glance at Amanda. "What a lucky friend. Follow me."

Amanda gritted her teeth. Did every woman in the hospital have a crush on Jake? Certainly every woman they passed in the lobby stared at him, stars in their eyes. He remained unperturbed and focused on helping her.

Luckily, she got right in to one of the emergency room doctors, who upon initial examination confirmed the dislocation.

"I'm going to reset this shoulder and then we'll get x-rays to see if anything is broken. It doesn't feel like you've got a break, but you may have torn your rotator cuff or labrum. We may need an MRI too." Dr. Jeung was a soft-spoken older woman, with a reassuring air.

"Thank you Doctor. Is someone coming in to help you reset it?" The woman was more slender than she was. Was she strong enough?

"I'll do it. Are you ready? It's going to hurt like hell, but it will be quick."

"Ready as I'll ever be." Amanda braced herself and held her breath.

Dr. Jeung moved quickly and snapped Amanda's shoulder back into place. Black dots swam in front of her eyes and she screamed loud enough to pierce her eardrums and probably every eardrum within a twenty-mile radius.

"Ms. McNeill, keep breathing. Stay with me. The pain will pass quickly." The tiny medieval torturer sounded like they were partaking in afternoon tea as opposed to having just inflicted the most pain Amanda had ever endured.

She inhaled deeply and forced herself to exhale slowly. Repeated the process. When her brain actually started to function again, a strange realization hit her. The stabbing pain was gone. Her shoulder still throbbed, but nothing like how she'd felt before Dr. Jeung set it.

"Okay. You're right. And how are you so incredibly strong?"

"Well, I work out with weights and I go to this army-style boot camp class. I'm stronger now than I was in my twenties." Dr. Jeung grinned at her. She wasn't a day less than fifty-five and could kick Amanda's ass.

"That's amazing. You're an inspiration. I need to get stronger."

"I agree. No question anyone would have been bruised and banged up, but in your line of work, it would be a good idea to start lifting weights. Don't blame yourself. You work with quarter horses—huge, strong animals.

Let's get you in for an MRI as soon as possible. If you've torn some ligaments or tendons, we should take care of it sooner than later. You can't go back to your usual work until we're sure what the extent of the damage to your shoulder is." Dr. Jeung's deceptively delicate hands tapped some notes into an electronic tablet.

"But it's breeding season and my schedule is incredibly demanding for the next several months. I don't have time to be injured." Amanda frowned.

"Well, if you don't get this taken care of now, you might miss a lot longer. Sit tight and I'll see if radiology can get you in and save you another trip down here." Dr. Jeung patted her good shoulder.

"Okay." Amanda forced herself to answer in a measured, calm tone. She'd keep herself together, although her shoulder ached. Damn it, she didn't have time for this nonsense.

Oh shoot, *time*. Sam would be home Sunday from her mini-honeymoon. No way could the ranch get through breeding season without Amanda's help. She pulled out her phone and sighed. How much should she admit? If she weren't such a wimp, she probably would have just gotten some bruises and scrapes from Cowgirl's kick. Mortifying. Talk about taking her safety for granted with her old mare.

In her profession, she couldn't afford to be complacent. She rubbed her left arm, which had thankfully settled down to a dull ache. She wouldn't bother Sam on her honeymoon––her sister would be worried about her and the state of the ranch. Seriously, what type of equine vet got kicked by a horse she'd owned almost her whole life?

Before Amanda could set the phone back into

her bag, Dylan called.

"So I called Sam and she and Holt will cut their honeymoon short and get home tonight instead of tomorrow. Everything will be fine." Dylan said.

Amanda jolted in the hard plastic seat, jostling her shoulder in the process. Stabbing pain shot down to her elbow. "Damn it, Dylan. Why would you do that? Call her back and tell her to absolutely not cut her honeymoon short."

"Amanda. You cursed?" Dylan gasped.

Amanda grimaced. She'd cursed at her sensitive, sweet, younger sister exactly zero times ever. But she was already miserable and didn't need to feel guilty for cutting Sam's honeymoon short. Amanda refused be responsible for her losing time with her new husband.

"I'm sorry. I'm hurting right now, but I'll be fine. There's no need to ruin the last night of Sam's honeymoon. I'll feel terrible for the rest of my life if you don't. Please call her back, for me." Yelling didn't work with Dylan, but guilt certainly did and Amanda didn't hesitate to employ the technique.

"If you're sure. I just thought––"

"I know your heart is in the right place, but I'll be fine. Owen and Marco have everything under control right now. Sam almost didn't take a mini-honeymoon because of the ranch. Let's give Sam a few more days because she'll be working twenty-four-seven soon. Okay?"

"Okay. I'll call her back now."

"Yes. Go. I'll be fine. I'm waiting on an MRI

and hopefully it won't take too long."

"I'll be home waiting for you. And don't be mad, but Dad and Angela asked if they should come straight there or meet back at the ranch."

Amanda groaned. "Seriously? Next you'll be telling me that you called our brothers."

Dylan hesitated. "I was about to. I'm sure they'll want to help out, and although Grant's still in Europe, Ryan and Austin aren't too far away."

"Don't you dare." She ground out the words.

"Look, Amanda, you have a family who loves you and you've always taken care of us, so just deal with it."

Before she could respond, a smiling nurse practitioner entered the room to escort her to radiology for her MRI. "Gotta go."

The cacophony from the MRI machine certainly didn't soothe her pounding headache, but at least it didn't take too long. Unfortunately, she'd have to wait at least forty-eight hours for the results.

Jake rose from the waiting room chair, his skin pale under his olive skin. Despite the pain, her heart knocked against her ribs and she smiled. How she could feel like flirting in her current condition was a testament to the fact Jake Cruz was smoking hot. He'd basically saved the day and taken care of her. Whether he'd slipped into paramedic mode and treated every injured person with the same calm, competent strength she didn't know, but hopefully he didn't carry everyone in his arms. Accustomed to always being the caretaker, Amanda had to admit she could become used to being taken care of by him.

Her left arm in a sling and a prescription for painkillers in her purse, Amanda insisted on walking to Jake's truck, eschewing the wheelchair. He helped her into the truck and she bit down hard on the inside of her lip to stifle a groan. Bruises were springing up like weeds in Angela's vegetable garden and her body felt like a pro boxer had used her for punching bag practice.

When she'd envisioned this afternoon with Jake, she'd pictured a day filled with long glances and flirtatious banter. If and when his powerful arms wrapped around her, it would be so they could passionately kiss. Instead, she'd been sobbing in pain, not moaning with pleasure. She sighed and stared at the scenery whizzing by out the window.

Jake may have had a crush on her in high school, but now he probably saw her in the same light as Stella, another rescue.

# CHAPTER 5

"YOU'RE THE PRETTIEST GIRL IN the world." Jake stroked Stella's furry belly. "Well, except for Amanda." He grinned down at the dog, who lounged in the fancy orthopedic dog bed he'd bought for her the first day he brought her home. Along with shiny food and water bowls, a banana-yellow stuffed chicken toy, tennis balls, and an enormous bone. Stella would be spoiled rotten when she was with him. Not like she wouldn't be spoiled rotten running around on the McNeills' two-hundred acre ranch. Though running wasn't in her future until she was completely healed.

Speaking of healing, his thoughts returned to Amanda. Although he recognized she needed to be in her own bed at home, he'd wanted to be the one fussing over her, the one to make her dinner, and the one to tuck her under the sheets. She'd been silent on the ride to her house and he'd been tempted to bring her back to his apartment. Tempted to take charge and carry her up the stairs. Tempted to press his mouth against her soft pink lips and carry her to his bed. Even when she wasn't at her best, he couldn't quell his desire for her. Leaving her at the ranch had been brutal.

He blew out a breath and shoved back his sleeves. No more procrastinating——time to open the emails from his sociology instructor and his school advisor. Bile rose in his throat and the old familiar dread in his gut cautioned him he'd screwed up his first exam. No matter how prepared he thought he'd been, he couldn't shake the feeling he'd blown it.

Failure. His greatest fear.

Luckily, throughout the course of his firefighting career, he'd managed to mix in the written exams with the practical ones, where he kicked ass. The fire captain who'd brought him on to the station had said he'd rather have someone who was quick on his feet, able to perform well under extreme pressure and do the job, than someone who looked perfect on paper and choked in the field. He'd excelled in school, but every single written test had been hell for him.

He massaged the back of his stiff neck and pushed to his feet. Jake marched over to his desk, feeling like he was on a mission to cross Death Valley in August and about as appealing. He sat down, counted to ten, and fired up his laptop.

Nobody was paying attention except for Stella, so he needed to open the emails and deal with the consequences. It was Intro to Sociology, for god's sake, not quantitative physics or calculus. Although anything that required him to read and write under any time constraints was challenging.

He could do this.

Jake gripped the edge of his mahogany desk, willing himself to hold on and breathe. *Do not throw laptop across the room.* No matter how satisfying it would feel to hear it hit the wall and shatter into a million little pieces. He exhaled an unsteady breath, let go of the solid wood, and scrubbed his hands through his hair.

Despite reviewing his notes more times than he cared to admit, he'd failed his first college exam. Officially. Not just a poor grade, but an actual "F." Not exactly a promising beginning to his path to fire captain. Staccato drumbeats pounded in his temples and he looked around his apartment, as if somehow something in the 925-square-foot space would provide an answer.

No response from the kitchen cabinets or the couch or the frickin' television. He rose from the chair and stalked around the room, willing his brain to activate. What would he do if the school decided they'd made a mistake admitting him and booted him from the program? He'd just have to wait until they told him in the video calls they'd requested. Great.

If getting his B.S. weren't an option, he'd need a new life plan. Not that being a firefighter wasn't his dream job. It was. But he needed to do something more. Like his big brother Rafael, with his M.B.A. and career as a financial whiz.

Rafael had always excelled in school and broke boundaries. Their dad practically worshiped the ground his brother walked on. Not that his dad wasn't proud of him too, but he'd always put the brothers in their respective slots. Rafael was the "smart, ambitious one" and Jake was the "big, strong one."

Well, those labels sucked. And he'd been chafing to prove everyone wrong since he was a kid. The only way he could figure out to do that, at least in his dad's eyes, was to be fire captain. That was the highest rank he could achieve, short of working to be fire chief, and no way in hell did he want a prominent public role. He loved the day to day of his job, loved working with the guys on his team, even though he didn't hang out with them often outside of work, and he certainly didn't want to get stuck working behind a desk.

No way in hell.

So he would do whatever it took to make this work. He would convince the school this failing grade was a one-off and it would never happen again. With a decisive nod, he sat and scheduled the calls with both his advisor and his teacher. They had to listen to him. Hopefully he could figure out what to say first.

He paused in front of the huge living room window, which usually bathed the room with natural light. Tonight, the darkness pouring in was as gloomy as his mood. He leaned his forehead against the cool glass, willing it to soothe the thundering in his temples.

Failing out wasn't an option. How could he fix this?

His phone flashed and he snatched it up.

*Hey bro, in the neighborhood and swinging by. Mom*

*gave me something to drop off. Be there in 5.*

Shit. Damn. Hell. He'd hoped Amanda was checking in with him. Not Rafael, his perfect older brother. His perfect smart graduate-degree-holding brother.

No way could Rafe learn he was in school. Especially not now. Rafael would want to help, but his brother was too damn intelligent and impatient with it. Back when they were kids, Rafael tried to help him but never understood why Jake couldn't grasp things as fast. Not that he was a dick about it, usually.

Jake slammed the computer shut and scooped up the Sociology textbook. The evidence of school needed to be stuffed somewhere, pronto. He glanced around and headed toward the kitchen, ready to stuff his supplies into a lower cabinet. Out of sight.

He crouched down and whipped open the cabinet by the stove and started to drag out the cast iron skillet and double-boiler he used to steam his vegetables. His brother would have no reason to rifle through his cabinets. Banging on the front door jolted him out of his contemplation. Damn his brother for texting three minutes before he showed up.

Stella jumped up out of her cushy bed and barked like a security dog.

"Coming. Hold on." Jake leapt up and looked around his apartment. He ran over and slammed the laptop shut. When his brother knocked again, he knew he didn't have time to flip on the television and pretend he'd been watching a game.

He caught Stella's collar, murmured comforting words, and brought her with him to the door. Immediately, she quieted and stood sentry by his side, her tail at half-mast.

He opened the door and greeted his brother, who immediately looked at Stella. "When did you get a dog?"

"It's a long story. Come on in. What do you have?" He stepped aside.

Rafael strolled in, carting a large foil covered dish. His brother was almost as tall as he was at 6'4, but was leaner and rangier. Probably because he wore a suit and worked in an office all week long. To say they were opposites wasn't far off.

Where Rafe was always top of the class in school, all the way through to earning his MBA from Harvard, Jake struggled with any type of academics. Where Rafe was charming and confident in any situation from Wall Street to dating supermodels, Jake was self-assured at work, but was more the quiet observer in his personal life. He loved his brother, but he'd never been able to stop himself from making the comparison and he never won the contest.

Rafe plopped the foil-covered dish on the coffee table, threw himself down on the large L-shaped grey couch, and flashed his straight white teeth. "Dad's been cooking again and you know mom always thinks you don't get enough to eat." He snorted. "I mean, does she even look at you? You're like a linebacker."

"Hey, man, I've got to stay fit for work. Not my fault you work in an office and sip lattes all day and go to Pilates instead of the weight room."

Rafe chuckled. "Pilates and lattes, right. You're hilarious. But seriously, what's with the mutt?"

Stella had remained glued by his side. He stroked her soft fur and sank onto the couch. "Stella got hit by a car that took off and I rescued her."

His brother frowned. "Seriously? Where are her owners?"

"Amanda thinks she's been abandoned—"

Rafe held up one hand. "Whoa. Who is Amanda? Do I know her?"

*Shit.* "She's the vet I took Stella to right after the accident. We're kind of sharing fostering."

"You're fostering the dog with the vet? What, is she hot?" Rafe waggled his eyebrows.

"Dude, seriously?"

"Just seems a little odd, but the dog is pretty cute. C'mere, girl." His brother reached out a hand and Stella trotted over and nuzzled him.

Jake ran his tongue around his teeth. At least they weren't discussing him going back to school. He'd discuss Stella all night long. But he needed to study.

"So why are you delivering food to me on a Saturday night?" He stood and grabbed the food dish and headed toward the kitchen. Maybe his brother would grab a hint?

His brother kept his gaze locked on the dog. "Just a quiet weekend, that's all. Isn't there a game on tonight? I could hang with you and catch up?"

"Sorry, early shift tomorrow and I'm dropping off the dog first."

Rafe frowned. "You trying to get rid of me?"

"I've just got stuff to do. Can't you find a last-minute date?"

Rafe leaned back against the couch cushions and crossed his arms. "Nah, don't feel like it. But is this Amanda cute?"

Damn it. His brother was a pest. "Look, she's the vet up at Pacific Vista Ranch."

"Pacific Vista Ranch?" Rafe's head whipped up to stare at him. "The McNeills' place?" Everyone knew who they were, especially after the paparazzi drama last summer.

"Yeah." Please go away now.

Rafe scratched at the scruff on his chin. "Wait a minute. I seem to recall a certain Amanda McNeill who you crushed on. Your high school tutor, right?"

Jake's jaw fell open. How the hell did his brother remember that? "The same. I didn't crush on her." *Liar.*

"I distinctly recall you coming home after tutoring sessions with glazed eyes and drool at the corner of your lips. Gorgeous blonde, right? Is she single?"

Jake squared his shoulders. No way in hell. "You aren't her type."

"Really?" Rafe drawled out the world and shifted on the couch to face him. "And you are?"

"Look, I've got stuff to do." He busied himself shoving the dish into the refrigerator.

His brother smirked. "Maybe I need a dog? Why don't I take Stella home tonight and I can take her to Amanda tomorrow. You're busy, right?"

Jake's ground his back teeth together and counted to three. "So go adopt one from the shelter. Stella's mine." *And I want Amanda to be mine too.*

His brother rose from the couch and crossed the open floor plan to join him in the kitchen. "Fine. I can take a hint. I'm going." He thumped him on the back.

"Sorry. You in town for a while or traveling a lot?" He usually enjoyed his brother's frequent visits. Just not so much tonight.

"I'm in New York meeting with some private equity guys this week. But maybe we can grab a drink or something in town over the weekend."

His brother lived in a huge mansion about fifteen miles south, high atop Mount Soledad, in La Jolla. "Sure. This time just give me some warning."

"Okay. Well, don't forget to tell mom you got the dish or she'll skin me." With that, his brother finally left.

The cords in his neck finally softened and he exhaled a deep breath. Would Amanda like Rafe? Every other woman in Southern California considered the *San Diego Magazine* 40 under 40 entrepreneur superstar the most eligible bachelor around. He couldn't worry about it now.

Wait a minute—Amanda. Amanda was brilliant. She'd been the one person who gave him confidence he could succeed in high school, under the right circumstances and with the right study methods. Maybe she would tutor him again.

And wouldn't that be an amazing excuse to spend time with her?

"Shit." When she'd been his tutor, she'd had certain subjects she tutored. He could bet they wouldn't be the ones in the Emergency Management Bachelor's degree. He stalked to the refrigerator, pulled out a gallon jug, and chugged some ice water. She'd graduated school three years before he did and the odds were she hadn't tutored anyone since then. How could he ask her to help him in subjects she hadn't taken and mastered?

Unless.

Unless she just helped him be more organized and gave him some tools on how to study more effectively. She was an expert at being a good student. At this point, he'd take anything he could get. He couldn't afford to hire someone from the outside, not with the already high college expenses. Nor could he pay Amanda, but it wasn't like the McNeills needed money.

What could he offer her in return for tutoring?

He could offer to help with some of the physical tasks of her job while she recuperated. He didn't know much about horses, but he was strong. Maybe he could help out on the ranch in some way.

His rubbed his jaw and pondered. Would it ruin any chance of them exploring the attraction simmering between them? Make her see him as a student and not a man? Were those teenaged dreams of her really viable?

His shoulders sagged and he exhaled an unsteady breath. She was a genius and he wasn't exactly a brainiac. She was wealthy and he was middle class. She'd achieved her dreams and he had four long years of school before he could even apply to become a fire captain.

Until he felt like an equal, he needed to focus on improving himself. Despite the cost. He would have to choose between having her help him fulfill his dreams or helping him fulfill his dreams of her. So how was he going to broach this conversation? He had another twenty-four-hour shift at work and could possibly come up with something before Monday.

Damn it. Maybe he could have had a chance with Amanda, but he had to be smart and choose his career.

# CHAPTER 6

"I'LL BE FINE, EVERYONE. I'M just bruised. Please don't fuss." Amanda fought the urge to scream and run to hide in her bedroom. Over the years, she'd sometimes resented her family assuming she was always fine. She'd wondered what it would be like to have everyone eager to take care of her.

Now she knew.

She despised it with a passion.

Angela, her beloved stepmom, clucked at her and rearranged the thin blanket around her shoulders again. "You got cow-kicked and tossed by a horse today, dislocated your shoulder, and spent hours in the ER. You will allow us to take care of you for once and not another word, do you hear me?"

Amanda sighed. She'd been nestled into the huge couch in the family room since Jake had brought her home from the hospital. Dylan hadn't left her alone for a second and now her dad and Angela were back from L.A. What she wouldn't give for Jake's quiet strength and support.

"Do you realize what could have happened?"

Chris McNeill, her overprotective father, frowned. "Now how long did the doctor tell you to take off from work?"

Amanda shrugged her good shoulder. "Yes, I realize. I screwed up and learned my lesson. I'm just banged and bruised. We won't know if anything is torn until the MRI results are ready, but I think I'm okay. I may need some help this week though." *Damn it.* Sam couldn't bear the brunt of breeding season without her.

"Well, I'm here and I can step in and help. But yes, maybe we should call in Dr. Dunmore until you're feeling like yourself." Her dad's thick eyebrows drew together.

Amanda grimaced. "Maybe." What if Dunmore screwed up the perfect system she and Sam had developed over the last six years?

"I just wish we'd been home today. I hate thinking of any of my girls getting hurt and me not being here." The tell-tale tic in her dad's jaw appeared.

Angela rose from the couch and joined Chris on the loveseat facing Amanda.

"She had a hunky fireman save the day. You should have seen him carry her into the house." Dylan piped in and fanned her hand in front of her face.

Amanda glared at her sister. And now she was trussed up like a chicken on the couch with no way to evade the next discussion.

"What was a hunky fireman doing at the ranch?" Angela's eyes widened.

Amanda sighed and filled them in on the events of the past few days. "So, Jake and I are sharing fostering of Stella. How do you guys feel about having a dog again? She's a doll."

"I'd love to have a dog again. I've missed the company since Kola died. But what's this about sharing her? Does this guy want her too?" Her dad asked.

"Well, he saved her and she's with him now. But his schedule is hectic so I don't think he can have a dog full-time." Amanda glanced down at her hands, willing the flush rising in her cheeks not to betray her. Her dad could read her like nobody else and her attraction to Jake was none of his business.

"Don't those guys work around the clock? Wouldn't the ranch be a better home for Stella?" Her dad asked.

Exhaustion rolled through Amanda in a long slow wave and she lifted her hands up to stop the deluge. "Guys, hold on. I'd say it is up to him. He's bringing her back in the morning."

She tugged at the blanket with her right hand. Time for bed, where she could replay Jake's powerful arms cradling her against his broad chest. Without the speculating gazes of her family.

Before this afternoon's catastrophe, Amanda had been positive she and Jake were close to hooking up. Fireworks sparked every time they were together. He was the perfect man for a fling—gorgeous, sweet, married to his job—just the ticket to shake off her boring life. They'd dive into a passionate affair, but be able to stay friends because the expectations would be clear.

Darn Cowgirl for throwing a wrench into her first potential romance in years.

"Are you having trouble standing? Do you need me to help you upstairs?" Dylan asked.

Shoot, had she been ruminating about jumping Jake's bones in front of her parents? "No. I can walk just fine. It's my shoulder, not my legs."

"Well, if you're sure." Dylan frowned.

"What about some help getting ready for bed?" Angela called.

Thankful her back was to the room, Amanda rolled her eyes. Being taken care of wasn't quite how she'd anticipated it would be. "No, thanks so much and good night, everyone."

She hobbled her bruised, sore self to the other wing of the house and up the stairs to her room. Maybe she'd exaggerated a bit when she'd assured everyone she was fine. Every muscle and bone in her body screamed in protest. She hated taking painkillers, but tonight she'd make an exception and continue with the prescription. Sleep would be a blessed relief.

And despite her embarrassment at Jake finding her sprawled out like a sack of oats, she couldn't wait to see him at 7 a.m. tomorrow.

Jake parked his truck in front of the majestic entrance to the McNeills' home. Unlike the first time when he'd rolled up with Stella wrapped up and bleeding, the dog perched on the front seat, enjoying the view and the breeze. Her pink tongue lolled out the side of her mouth and she turned to grin at him. As her injuries healed and her trust in humanity was restored, Stella's personality was shining through. Although the impertinent side that enjoyed stealing his socks and sleeping with them could possibly quiet a bit.

"Ready to check into the Ritz, sweet girl?"

Stella's ears perked up and he could swear she'd nodded when she turned to look at him.

"Okay, let's do this." He walked around to the passenger side and lifted the dog into his arms. She wasn't ready to jump down from the truck at this point. No way would he risk Stella taking foolish chances with her recovery. Although she acted like she was fine, the accident was still too fresh in his mind.

Kind of like Amanda's accident. He placed Stella on the ground. Together, they headed to the enormous wooden front door. Before he could knock, it swung open and Amanda stood in the doorway.

"Good morning." Amanda smiled at him and leaned down to caress Stella's head with her good hand.

Damn, she was beautiful. His heart pounded against his ribcage and every particle of moisture evaporated from his throat. He swallowed and gazed down at the curve of her long slender neck and her shiny golden ponytail. A white tank top didn't hide the bruises marring her creamy skin or the sling supporting her left arm. How had he not seen all those marks yesterday?

He frowned. "You're really hurt and you should be in bed." He couldn't ask her for a favor now, not when she looked borderline fragile, with her delicate collarbones and slender frame.

Amanda pushed to her feet. "Not you too. My family would wrap me in cotton wool for a month if they had their way. I'm fine."

Jake shook his head. "I think you downplayed your injuries yesterday. Those bruises are just bad. Any news on the MRI?"

Her full lips flattened and her thick fringe of lashes hid her emerald gaze. "The bruises look worse than they are. It's Sunday morning, so no on the MRI."

And now he was irritating her. Definitely not ideal timing to ask her to tutor him. "Sorry. I just hate seeing you in pain, that's all."

Amanda gazed at him. "Don't apologize. I'm just frustrated and I obviously don't handle being injured well." One corner of her lips quirked up.

He nodded and smiled back. "I'd go nuts if I couldn't do my job. I don't blame you. But are you okay to keep the dog?"

She shrugged her good shoulder. "My family is home and they are excited. Stella will be treated like a princess. She looks pretty happy right now."

Stella's tail thumped and she leaned against Amanda's long legs. They both laughed and reached to pet her at the same time. Amanda's slender fingers brushed against his and she gasped, but unlike last time that happened, she didn't pull away. For a few moments, they both scratched the dog's silky head and Stella's entire lower body wagged along with her tail.

Jake's fingers itched to shift those last few inches and catch Amanda's hand in his. He was close enough to catch her fresh scent and all he had to do was clasp her hand and tug her into his arms. Stella wasn't the only one feeling happy right now. Or excited. Every muscle in his body was on high alert. Damn it, he didn't want to be her student, he wanted to be her lover.

His pulse was racing, but he managed to respond. "She was great. We had a wild Saturday night. But I'm concerned about you."

Her high cheekbones suffused with pink. "I'm stronger than I look, but you're right, even though my shoulder isn't too bad, my head is killing me. I think maybe I should rest today after all."

His shoulders softened and he gestured to her sling. "Are you sure there's nothing I can do to help?"

She shook her head, her shiny ponytail swinging. "You're sweet. Like I said, I may hit the couch and watch Netflix all day."

"Well, rest up. I'm on every other day until Friday. Is it cool if I take her for the weekend?" Damn, he needed to come up with a reason to see her before the end of the week. He couldn't ask her about school over the phone.

"Oh you can't see her until Friday? I thought you'd take her every other day?" Her eyes widened.

His breath lodged in his throat. "I could come by Wednesday?" Maybe he could figure out a way to have it all: ask her to tutor him and ask her out. She was too beautiful, too special and too perfect to let slip through his fingers. He'd beaten more formidable odds.

She smiled and her face lit up. "Well, Sam will be back and I'll have to take it easy with work. We could take Stella for a walk around four?"

When she smiled at him like that, he'd jump off a bridge if she asked. He grinned. "Perfect. I'll text you when I'm on the way. Gotta run."

"Thanks again Jake. I'll see you then." The smile remained on her face.

He turned to leave, paused, and looked back. "Will you please let me know what the MRI says?"

"Sure." She waved, guided Stella inside the house, and shut the door.

Jake strode to his car, adrenaline pumping through his veins. Amanda McNeill, the woman he'd dreamed of for years, had smiled at him just the way he'd imagined. Interest gleamed in her green eyes, chemistry crackled between them, and she clearly wanted to spend time with him. Hell, maybe she was nice to everyone, but he wasn't imagining that glow in her eyes.

He hopped up into his truck, gripped the steering wheel, and closed his eyes. Damn it. When he'd been with her just now, it had been too easy to postpone asking her to tutor him. Too easy to bask in her presence, to savor the simple enjoyment of her company. Too easy to forget his priorities.

And there was the problem: if he was going to get promoted at some point, he needed to get his act together. Said act included studying and staying on schedule, taking and passing the damn tests in the prescribed time limits, and sucking it up. No pressure. School had to come first.

So here he was. A twenty-four-hour shift ahead of him and time to ponder what the hell to do. Was there any possible way he could have it all? He turned on the ignition and drove off the McNeill grounds. To ever be worthy of someone like Dr. Amanda McNeill, he needed to be the best he could be. And to do that, she needed to be his tutor, not his girlfriend. He'd have to ask for help and not ask for a date.

# CHAPTER 7

AMANDA GRIMACED AT HER REFLECTION in the bathroom mirror. "Thanks for helping me with my hair. It's going to be a long month at this rate."

Dylan stood behind her wielding a blow dryer and round brush. "Well, this is a special occasion because you're seeing the sexy fireman. I'll whip it into a ponytail for you the rest of the time you need it. Are you sure you feel up to seeing him?"

Amanda cursed under her breath. "I am fine. But getting ready is tougher than I imagined." The MRI had revealed she had partial tears in her rotator cuff and her labrum, which made lifting her arm overhead excruciating. Although she didn't have to keep wearing the annoying sling, her doctor recommended physical therapy and lots of rest. Two luxuries that didn't mesh with the intensity of breeding season. Healing required something she was short on: time.

"I bet." Dylan's eyes were wide. "You look gorgeous. Do you need help getting dressed? No way are you wearing that green hoodie again."

"What's wrong with my hoodie?" Well, she

had been wearing it for the last three days. She pouted. "It's really hard to pull anything over my head. But you're right."

"What about one of your flannel shirts? Those are always cute with jeans."

Dylan followed Amanda into her walk-in closet. "You're right. I'll get fancy with the gray and pink plaid." She needed all the confidence she could get.

"So have you guys been talking or texting or anything?"

"Not really, just to confirm the time. I think when he's working, he's out of pocket." At least that's what she figured. What she hoped.

"I'm sure. Well, I need to get back to my studio. You two lovebirds have fun. I still think you're soul mates and now he's old enough to handle you." Dylan blew her a kiss from the bedroom doorway.

Amanda laughed. "Oh please. You and your romantic little heart go create the next great masterpiece." Her talented sister poured her emotions onto canvas and was on track to achieve massive success in the art world.

Amanda finished dressing with gritted teeth. She was still sore and the bruises covering her left side looked like she was the love child of a purple Dalmatian and a Holstein cow. Her fingers curled into fists. This whole accident was a wake-up call.

One: never ignore the horse's signals or take safety for granted. She sighed because she knew better. Two: she needed to start lifting weights.

No more willowy wispy Olive Oyl arms for her. She'd never been a gym person—this would be a whole new adventure. Dr. Jeung's fitness inspired her to become the strongest she could be. But when she'd wished for some changes in her monotonous routine, being sidelined with an injury hadn't been what she had in mind.

She'd envisioned long walks with the sexiest man she'd ever met and the cutest dog she'd seen in years. Hoped he'd overcome the sweet shyness she could see beneath the surface and act on his boyhood crush. She'd been sure he was interested in her judging by the gleam in those intense obsidian eyes—it couldn't all be for Stella, could it? Now, she wasn't so sure.

And suddenly, she very much wanted to be involved with Jake Cruz. His stoic strength simultaneously made her feel safe and excited. His sheer size made her want to snuggle up in his arms. His sheer size made her want to slide her arms around his lean waist, and melt into his broad, muscular body. Tilt her head back and kiss those lips, which were almost too pretty and full to belong on his masculine face.

Would he get over his shyness and ask her out today? And if he didn't ask, could she overcome her own reticence?

Glancing at the clock on her dressing table, she realized Jake was arriving any minute. Her stomach churned. Taking charge at work was as natural as breathing. Taking charge in her personal life? Not so much. But if he didn't ask her out, she would take the lead. Jake Cruz didn't stand a chance against a determined woman ready to embark on a passionate affair.

Jake wiped his sweaty palms on his jeans and knocked on the enormous front door. Back when he'd put her on a pedestal, he never imagined he'd actually be able to speak to Amanda McNeill without stammering and sweating. Now they'd met as adults, he'd been certain destiny had stepped in and given him a chance with the woman of his dreams.

He'd blown his chance to date her. He couldn't think of a soul who could help him study and earn the most important piece of paper for his life plan. Certainly nobody at the station. Definitely not his brother. Not receiving his degree and squandering his chance for promotion wasn't an option.

The door whipped open. Instead of the most beautiful girl in the world, a broad shouldered reddish-haired man stared at him from almost eye level.

"You must be the dog-rescuing fireman. I'm Chris McNeill." He reached out and gave Jake a firm handshake.

"Jake Cruz. Nice to meet you, sir." The man demanded respect, not just from his sheer physical presence, but his accomplishments in the entertainment and the horse breeding industries.

"Come on in, Stella's in the kitchen and Amanda should be down any second." He headed down the large high-ceilinged hallway. "So, how's fire season looking this year?"

Jake relaxed—a topic where he was an expert. "All the rain we're having should help. We're almost out of the drought for the first time in seven years."

"Excellent news."

The minute they entered the kitchen, Stella leapt up from a scarlet-colored dog bed and trotted over to greet them. Jake crouched down and the dog rushed into his arms and proceeded to bathe his face in kisses.

"Hi, girl." He laughed.

"I see Stella's happy to see you." Amanda said from behind him.

When he turned, his breath caught in his throat. She stood silhouetted in the large doorway, her golden hair tumbling around her face in soft waves, beckoning him to run his fingers through it. Her smile was shy, lighting up her delicate face and tip-tilted green eyes. She wore faded jeans, boots, and a flannel over a thin, white tank top. Somehow, she still looked like royalty. "Hey there."

Amanda joined them and reached down to scratch Stella's ears. The dog leaned into him, but craned her head up to enjoy Amanda's petting.

"It looks like the dog definitely loves her rescuers. She's fitting in around here really well," Chris said.

"Yeah, she's a sweet girl." Jake caught himself before he grimaced. Of course this was a much more suitable home for the dog. A family, acres to run and play on, horses, and probably whatever her little heart desired. But he didn't want to let her go either, and not just because of Amanda.

Amanda smiled at him reassuringly. "Let's go take her for a walk. We've been making her take it pretty easy, just to be safe."

"Great. How's the shoulder and are you sure you shouldn't be using a sling?" Damn, way to sound like an overprotective parent or something.

"She's a stubborn one. Don't bring up her physical therapy schedule or work." Her dad commented from a breakfast nook by the far window. Jake had been so focused on Amanda he hadn't noticed when Chris crossed the room.

Amanda narrowed her eyes at her dad. "Me? Please. Compared to the rest of this family, I'm a saint."

Chris laughed. "You definitely are the McNeill saint. I don't know what I'd do without you to balance out the rest of us."

Amanda stiffened and Jake wouldn't have caught it if he hadn't been so close to her. Huh, so she didn't like her role as the saintly sister.

"Ready?" Jake addressed Amanda.

She turned and gave him a tight smile. "Stella's leash is in the foyer. And yes, you can have the honor."

"Nice to meet you, Mr. McNeill." Jake gave a half wave.

"You too, Jake. And call me Chris." He smiled and shifted his attention down to the newspaper on the table.

Jake grabbed the pink leash and together they stepped outside into the crisp morning air. A red-tailed hawk soared overhead. He wasn't going to ask what all the sainthood discussion referred to—he'd prefer to be on Amanda's good side and probing family dynamics might not be ideal.

They strolled together in comfortable silence. How awesome was it that she enjoyed the quiet and didn't feel the need to fill the air with words, just like him? Although between the two of them, they might just walk for miles without talking, and he needed to ask her about tutoring.

"So what happened with the MRI and the physical therapy?" With her bruises covered, she looked healthy and perfect.

Amanda sighed and looked up at him. "Well, some good news—I don't need surgery. I've got some partial rotator cuff and labrum tears, and have to do physical therapy for six weeks. And I'll admit it's hurting me. But the timing really stinks, you know?"

"No surgery is always good news. What about your job?" And he was asking all the questions her dad advised against, but he wanted to understand her situation.

Amanda frowned. "Well, Sam's adamant about me not working with the breeding or foaling."

"That makes sense until you're stronger. Can you still do some of it?"

She nodded. "Yes, there's a fair amount I can do, but it's more of the paperwork and lab work, as opposed to the hands-on. I'll need to have another vet come in to help Sam once the mares start foaling. That's one of my favorite parts of breeding season."

"Well, hopefully you'll heal faster than you think."

Jake tried not to gawk when they walked past a sparkling crystal blue Olympic-sized pool and a white-canopied cabana. Stella yanked on the leash, angling for the rippling turquoise water. "I bet Stella loves swimming."

The dog's ears perked up and Amanda laughed. "I bet she does, but not until all her wounds are healed."

"You two can heal up together."

Amanda shrugged one slender shoulder. "I guess. So this is Sam and Holt's house. It's one of three guest houses on the property."

The guest house looked more like a huge house to him, just like the stable. Everything seemed oversized here. "Nice. And you and your sister Dylan live in the main house with your parents?"

"Well, we are in separate wings, so it seems like we've got our own place except when it comes time for meals. But we're close, so it's all good."

They reached the peak of another rolling emerald green hill and Jake stopped, his mouth dropping open. "Is that seriously the Pacific? You've got an ocean view from the ranch?"

Her pink lips curved up. "Pretty amazing, right? Especially from five miles away. We're lucky."

"Yeah you are. Okay if I let Stella off leash

now?"

"Sure, go ahead."

Jake reached down and released the clasp, stroked Stella's head, and they all continued to walk together. "So, I wanted to ask you something." Sweat prickled on the back of his neck.

Amanda looked at him, her brows lifted, and her full lips curved up. "Sure."

"It's kind of awkward." He rubbed the back of his neck, willing his pulse to stop hammering.

"Don't be shy, just ask." Her smile broadened.

Encouraged by her apparent receptiveness, Jake asked, "Is there any way you could tutor me again?"

Amanda's smile vanished and she stopped in her tracks. "I'm sorry, what?"

*Shit.* "You know I'm back in school, right? I'm already not doing well and I figured…" He shrugged.

She tilted her head and studied him. "You know I haven't tutored anyone since college and that was just in certain subjects. I mean, what are you even majoring in?"

His heartbeat shifted up another gear to turbo speed. "Of course. It's just I'm a little desperate and you're the person who helped me feel confident enough in high school to finish. Sorry, didn't mean to bug you."

Amanda paused. "You're not bugging me. I just thought…" She leaned down and stroked Stella.

"Thought what?" Had she been feeling their connection and wanting him to ask her out?

She shook her head. "Nothing. Never mind. Don't you think you should find a tutor that's familiar with the subject matter? I don't think I'm that person."

"Well, I think it's less the subject matter and more I haven't really had to study for ten years. Well, except for the testing in fire school, but that was different."

"So, you're thinking more like how to get organized and plan your time to get it done?" She cocked her head to one side, not smiling now, but not frowning either.

He nodded. "Yeah. Since it takes me so much longer to actually process everything, maybe some help with scheduling my time so I don't end up skipping or failing another test."

"Failing another test?" She frowned.

"Yeah, I already failed my first test. Sociology of all things. Just ran out of time and tried to hurry through it. I can't let it happen again. I've got to get this degree." His stomach twisted into knots.

She considered. "Well, if I do help you, what do I get in return?"

He gulped. "Maybe I could help out at the ranch or do things for you while your shoulder is healing? I don't know much about horses, but…"

She shook her head. "We've got plenty of staff and I have to bring another vet in to handle some of my load for a while. But you might be able to help me too. You lift weights, right?"

His eyes widened. "Lift weights?"

She nodded. "Yeah, you know, work out. How

do you keep those muscles so…umm, strong?" Her cheeks were turning pink.

She'd noticed his muscles. Why did that make him want to flex his biceps and puff out his chest? "I do. Lift weights, run, rock climb, hike." Warmth crept into his own cheeks.

"Well, this whole nightmare situation got me thinking. I'm a fast runner and have endurance, but I don't have much strength. I mean, the doctor who set my shoulder back into place was tiny and probably could have picked me up and tossed me across the room. I want to be like her. I need to be stronger, but have no clue what to do."

She wanted to work out with him? An image of her in snug yoga pants and a fitted tank top flashed before him. Holy shit. He just stared at her and his mind blanked.

"Hello, Jake." She waved her hand in front of his face. "The doctor also recommended a weight-lifting program to build up my strength. I mean, my size has never been an issue, it's not like I have to pick up the horses or anything, for god's sakes. I need more muscle, you know, so if I have another run in with a misbehaving horse, it wouldn't be such a big deal."

Jake couldn't shake the visual of Amanda's creamy skin and long limbs glistening with effort.

She huffed out a breath. "What do you think of a trade? I help you study and you help me get stronger?"

"Um, don't you have to do physical therapy first? I mean, with your shoulder?" He finally found his voice.

"Well, can't I do both? I mean I can work on getting my legs and core stronger, right? And maybe strengthen my right arm?" She crossed her arms.

"You've got a point. Sure, we can do some hikes and I'm sure I can come up with some workouts around your shoulder for now."

"I guess rock climbing isn't an option?" Her eyes twinkled and her lips hitched up at the corners.

He laughed. "Not exactly. Even if you hadn't hurt your shoulder, I'd want you to get stronger lifting weights before you started climbing."

"Are you calling me a wimp? I've just always preferred running or riding horses because I love being outside. But this was a wake-up call and if I'm going to continue my career, I need to get stronger, so weights it is."

"Sounds like a deal. Although I think I'm getting the easier side of it." If he could control his physical reaction to her anyway.

Amanda laughed and flexed a bicep. "Oh don't assume this will be easy. How's this for a muscle?"

He reached out and gently squeezed her arm through the flannel shirt. She jolted and electric sparks jolted his palm, but he tried to play it cool. "Hmmm…not bad, but we can definitely beef these up."

She drew her arm back down by her side, her face unreadable once again. Hell, she should play poker with her ability to look totally neutral. She had to have felt those sparks too. Without thinking, he stepped forward again and lifted his hands toward her waist to pull her close and suddenly remembered. He froze. Dropped his arms back by his sides.

He couldn't explore with a kiss or an embrace. The cost was too high. Now she'd agreed to his bargain, he had to keep their relationship platonic, at least until he was certain he could finish school. Maybe he could make a move once he'd settled back into school and was getting good grades. She wouldn't need to tutor him forever, right? Just for now.

For a moment, time stood still until Stella barked.

Amanda turned away. "Should we head back to the house?"

As they crossed the grassy hills, he asked, "Does Friday work for our first session?" *Please don't let her change her mind.*

"Sure. It's probably best if I come to you so I can see where you're studying and doing your schoolwork. I'll be free after four or so, depending on how the day goes." She was back to her crisp, no-nonsense teacher voice.

"Perfect. I'll be there. I can text you my address." He swallowed down the desire to touch her again. Touching her was dangerous.

They reached the front drive, where his truck was parked. He crouched down and rubbed Stella's ears and she promptly slathered his face with kisses. He stood and gave the leash to Amanda.

"Great. See you Friday." She gave him a small

smile and turned and headed to her door.

He trudged to his truck, his legs leaden and his stomach shaky. Although he'd convinced her to help him, he didn't feel an ounce of satisfaction. Out on those grassy hills, all he'd wanted was to wrap her in his arms and kiss her until the world disappeared. To see if she tasted as incredible as she looked.

Damn his learning challenges and all the ways they'd screwed up his life. For a few days, he'd actually believed he could have it all, even a relationship with Amanda McNeill.

# CHAPTER 8

JAW CLENCHED, AMANDA FORCED HER-SELF to casually stroll back into the house, like she wasn't devastated. How could she have misread Jake's intentions? One minute she was smiling and ready to suggest a romantic date spot and the next she had to draw on her greatest talent: her poker face.

With the palpable chemistry between them, she'd been confident in their mutual attraction. Even certain his youthful crush was still in place. When he'd asked for her to tutor him again, she'd hidden her disappointment and maintained her composure. She'd been positive he was going to ask her out on a date. Not ask for help.

Darn it, Jake was the man who'd shown up on her doorstep with an adorable dog, looking both heroic and mouthwateringly delicious. He'd been strong and sweet and totally tempting. The answer to her desire for something exciting to happen. She'd gathered her courage to ask him out and then, poof—her brilliant plan to seduce him evaporated.

Unless.

Unless he was more shy than she'd realized and this was his way of spending more time with her before taking their relationship to the next level. Why couldn't they study together and have a fling? Thank god for her quick recovery: asking him to help her work out had been quite inspired. What woman wouldn't want to see him in work-out clothes, sweating while miles of beautiful sinewy muscle flexed? She leaned against the front door and her eyelids fluttered shut.

Although she wasn't sure how much help she'd be with his course work, she was impressed his ego hadn't prevent him from asking for help. At least she could help him organize his workspace, give him some tips on time management, and offer encouragement. She'd been a great tutor back in the day, if she did say so herself. She'd do her best to help him in any way she could. The more time they spent together, the more time they could get closer. In every way.

"Penny for your thoughts."

Amanda's eyes popped open and she glanced around the foyer. "Oh hi."

"Everything okay?" Angela, her beloved step-mom, leaned against the doorjamb leading down the wide hallway.

"Fine. Just enjoying this sweet pup. I think she'll be a great addition to the clan."

The dog pressed up against Angela, who reached down to scratch behind her ears. "So the hunky fireman is giving up custody then?"

Heat crept up Amanda's cheeks. "He is awfully

handsome, you're right. No, he still wants to share her, although it makes sense for her to stay here most of the time. He did save her and she adores him."

"Makes sense. Dylan told me that you used to tutor him in high school. And that he'd had a big crush on you?" Angela quirked one dark eyebrow.

And her cheeks were flaming now. Darn her little sister. "I actually didn't recognize him because he was a scrawny little freshman."

Angela's dark eyes twinkled. "From what I saw out the window, there's nothing little about him now. Is he single?"

She ran her tongue around her teeth. "He is single and yes, he's huge and shy and sweet." How much did she want to share with her family? She valued her privacy immensely and who knew what would happen when they started spending more time together?

"Hmm. I was about to brew a pot of tea. Want to join me?" Angela started walking toward the kitchen, the dog close to her side.

Amanda exhaled. Trust Angela not to push her for details. "Sure. I'm meeting with Sam in about an hour. We're going to bring in Leo Dunmore to handle the breeding duties and I'll be stuck with the paperwork and whatever I can do in the lab."

"I think that's smart, even though I know it's hard for you to allow someone else to step in. Your dad can also help, but your health is a priority. So what's the rehab plan?"

Amanda sank into the comfy bench seat at the

breakfast nook. "Twice a week for six weeks, starting Monday. I'm hoping it won't take that long. I'm also supposed to ice it a few times a day."

Her stepmom crossed the kitchen to the freezer and whipped out a pre-made ice pack. Luckily, it had a Velcro fastening to stay in place. "Here you go. Put this on while I make the tea."

She strapped the irritating thing on her shoulder and told herself to suck it up. She could have had to have surgery or broken a bone. This injury was just a minor setback. *Maybe Jake hadn't asked her out because she was hurt?*

"Here's your tea. And let me repeat, penny for your thoughts." Angela slid into the chair across from her at the table.

She sniffed in the delicious bergamot fragrance. "My favorite, Earl Grey. Thanks so much." Amanda sipped her tea, savoring the exotic flavor. "Well, I have a plan. It's kind of a secret, and I'll tell you if you don't tell anyone else, especially my dad."

Her stepmom's eye's widened. "Secrets? Do they have anything to do with Jake by chance?"

Amanda looked around to make sure neither her dad nor her sisters were entering the kitchen. "Well, Jake asked me to help him study because he's getting his degree so he can be promoted to captain. And that is a secret. He doesn't want anyone to know until he's done."

"Really? Why on earth not? You're going to tutor him again? That's pretty cute."

Her belly fluttered in anticipation of seeing him

on Friday. "Right? I hope I can help him. So when he asked me, I told him I would tutor him if he helped me get stronger and work out."

"Hmmm…sounds like a *very* interesting arrangement. Good for you. So you like him, don't you?"

Heat rose in her cheeks and she nodded. Why not admit she was interested in him? Especially to Angela, who she trusted and loved.

Her stepmom beamed. "Well, he's handsome, saves dogs, fights fires, and probably is still nursing his high school crush on you. I say you have fun and enjoy yourself—you deserve it."

"We'll see. If nothing else, I'll get bigger biceps and he'll hopefully pass his next exam." She grinned. But wouldn't it be great if it turned into a steamy, spicy sexual adventure? Angela didn't need those details.

"Well I love it, honey. Just be careful of your shoulder until you've got the medical release, okay?"

"Of course." But her shoulder better heal fast. How could she seduce Jake with only one arm?

"That's not all though, is it?" Her stepmom sipped her tea.

Amanda shook her head. "Well, with Sam and Holt moving into the guest house and Dad dipping his toe back into the movie industry, it makes me question whether I've been in a rut."

Angela's dark eyes widened. "Really? Pacific Vista Ranch has definitely been a safe haven for you. Or are you worried about working with the horses?"

She shrugged her healthy shoulder. "I can't help but feel like if I'd been stronger, I wouldn't have gotten injured so badly. And working with Stella made me realize how much I love dogs. I was planning on contacting Dog Days Rescue and offering to volunteer. You know, vaccines, check-ups, etc."

Angela clapped her hands together. "What a wonderful idea. I think that would be great and you'd expand your circle beyond the ranch. But you have to wait until you're healed."

"I know and that's another reason I'm so frustrated with this injury. I'm finally making plans to try something new and now I have to wait." She sighed and stared into the tea, willing an answer to pop out of the steaming depths.

Angela laid one hand over hers. "Oh sweetheart, you've been the rock for your sisters and dad for so long. I've always worried about the burden you took on after your mom passed. It's not easy being the one everyone looks up to and counts on to be the steady one."

Amanda's eyes filled. "You always understand. I don't know what we'd have done without you. You've been our rock."

"Well, I try to be, but I've been hoping you'd allow yourself to let loose and go a little wild."

Amanda snorted through the tears running down her face. "Not exactly the wild McNeill sister."

"Well, Sam digs in her heels and Dylan isn't

tethered to the ranch with the horses, like you two. You can do whatever you want with your life. We can always hire an equine vet if you're done with it. You're the smartest person I know, so whatever you decide to do, you can achieve it."

Amanda wiped her face. Tears were not her usual M.O. "No, it isn't that I don't want to be a vet. I guess I just feel like I'm realizing I've been closed off to a lot of things and don't want to wake up and have let life pass me by."

"I understand. Well, maybe this injury was the universe's way of slowing you down to really ponder it. You've got the family behind you no matter what you do." Angela's warm brown eyes and broad smile emphasized her sincerity. "And working out with Jake is definitely not the request of someone in a rut."

Amanda's chest lightened. Friday, she'd wear her favorite jeans and bring over a bottle of wine, just to celebrate a successful night of studying. Jake might believe she was coming solely as his tutor, but looking her best couldn't hurt. She had plans for him.

# CHAPTER 9

JAKE RAN HIS HAND OVER his jaw and studied himself in the bathroom mirror. He'd showered, shaved, and scrubbed every surface in his apartment until it gleamed. The refrigerator was stocked with any and every type of snack item he could imagine so they wouldn't starve until if and when they ordered dinner in. Even if it wasn't a date, they could have dinner, right? Wouldn't that be the polite thing to do to thank her for helping him out? *Keep telling yourself that, buddy.*

He was as prepared as he'd been for his initial exercises during Emergency Medical Training, but he didn't recall his heart racing so much then. Nor were his muscles randomly twitching and snapping like they were now. He scanned the open floor plan apartment again and hurried over to adjust the dishtowel hanging next to the sink.

Like she'd inspect how neatly he folded his towels. He grimaced. What would Amanda think of his place? It was a great one-bedroom apartment, but it was light years away from a sprawling estate on two hundred plus acres. Worlds apart not just in their education, but also in their upbringing and lifestyle.

He double-checked that his books, notebooks, and sharpened pencils were neatly stacked next to his laptop on the wide, granite kitchen island. At first he'd thought to work at his desk, but when he'd sat down he realized they'd be too close together. Like, thighs and shoulders brushing together. Like, being able to smell the beachy scent emanating from her creamy skin and silky hair.

If they sat in such close proximity, he could guarantee his focus would not be on showing her the detailed outline he'd made with his notes or reviewing the semester's curriculum. He'd definitely be distracted and possibly unable to prevent himself from reaching out and touching her. Like he'd dreamed of doing when she'd been his high school tutor.

They'd have more space on barstools at the counter. Maintaining space was the smart way to set up the date, scratch that, the study session. Keep his eye on the end goal of achieving his leadership position. Keep his hands, lips, and every part of his body to himself.

A firm knock sounded at the door and he glanced around one more time. It was as good as it was going to get. He released an unsteady breath and went to let Amanda and Stella in. He opened the door and his chest tightened. Like it always did around her.

"Hi." Amanda smiled, a bottle of wine in one hand and Stella's hot pink leash in the other.

Amanda's blond hair was straight and silky over one shoulder and her delicate heart-shaped face was framed with a snug black turtleneck that emphasized her slender neck, narrow shoulders, and tiny waist. She wore faded jeans tucked into black boots and she looked incredible. He reached out for the wine bottle so he had something to do with his hands other than toss her over his shoulder and carry her off to his bedroom.

Stella launched herself over the threshold and rocketed into the apartment, tail spinning and wagging like a helicopter.

"Come on in. So I guess Stella's happy to be here." He'd stare at the dog so he could get his heart rate under control. He hoped.

Amanda laughed when Stella leaned up against her legs. "Every day she's feeling better. It's great. Once her fur returns, she'll be as good as new."

"Thanks to you." He smiled.

"No, thanks to you rescuing her. And nobody has claimed her, so I'd say she's ours." Amanda beamed.

He swallowed hard and glanced down at the bottle of wine gripped in his hand. His knuckles were white. "Great."

Unable to rip his gaze from hers, they stood for a moment without speaking. His pulse was most definitely not slowing down, not with her praising him and smiling at him with not just her lips, but with her sparkling green eyes. His brain screamed warnings at him to step away from the beauty and get his shit together. His feet remained rooted to the spot.

Amanda was not at his apartment on a date, she was there as a favor. His dream woman was there to help him with his education, not to spend the evening seducing him.

Stella barked and broke the spell between them. "Can I get you something to drink?"

Amanda shook her head. "No, I figure we could have a glass of wine after we get some work done, you know, earn the pleasure."

*Pleasure.* Every inch of him stiffened. Damn it, he could think of a million ways to pleasure her and not one had anything to do with a glass of wine. He turned toward the kitchen before he pulled her into his arms. "Let me put this in the refrigerator and we'll get started." *Study. School. Career. Focus.*

She crossed the room, Stella trotting along behind her. "Is this where you study?" She gestured toward all his materials on the counter.

"No, but there's more room here than at my desk." *And his jeans were suddenly really tight.*

"Okay, that makes sense. Ready to get started?" She pulled out a barstool and sat.

"Yeah." A flush crept up the back of his neck. Luckily she was already checking out his notebooks and he managed to slip onto the barstool and hide his body's reaction.

Even at the kitchen island, they were too close. Her fresh breezy scent surrounded him and her shiny hair was mere inches away from brushing against him. He sucked in a breath, held it, and turned to stroke Stella's furry head. *Crap.*

Stella's tail thumped on his wood floors. Focus on the dog, then the schoolwork. Nothing else.

Her tone turned brisk. "Maybe you should send Stella to bed so we can review your notes. We'll go from there."

Damn, her tutor voice sounded so sexy when she said "to bed." He swallowed, his throat basically drier than Southern California during the Santa Ana winds. And he should have grabbed a glass of water because he couldn't get up now without revealing his arousal.

"The blue notebook has my sociology notes and the brown hardback is the textbook." He managed to rasp the words out. Prayed he sounded casual.

She pulled both of them off of the stack and opened the notebook, revealing his meticulously printed notes. "Anything online for this class?"

"Well, the lectures are all online, some live and some recorded and I can listen to them whenever. There's some bullet-pointed information, but just on the screen. I prefer using the print."

She gestured for him to continue.

"The schedule is flexible because they're used to firefighters having unpredictable hours. So I have timeframes for completing tests and classes, but not exact dates."

"Now did you negotiate in extra time for accommodations?"

He nodded. Of course. Those requirements followed him through all academic institutions.

"Yeah, they're fully aware."

She nodded. "I think this kind of program is perfect for you because one of the issues you had was getting distracted taking tests in full classrooms or the time constraints. You do have extra time for tests, right?"

He frowned and looked down at the counter, the old sense of shame chilling his skin. "Yeah. Not that it helped."

He jolted when her smooth hand brushed his forearm. "Jake, you can do this. Don't forget that. It's all about the way you process, not about intelligence. You're really smart." Her green eyes glowed like a cat's.

He slid his arm out of reach and shrugged. He'd never be able to pay attention with her touching him. He needed her laser-sharp genius IQ, not her caresses. "I've never been accused of being smart, but I have to do this. Whatever it takes."

"Well, I'm telling you I think you are smart and brave and a total badass firefighter. You perform an elite service that most of the population couldn't handle or even dream of doing. Your parents must be really proud of you." Her lips curved into a sweet smile.

He shrugged again.

His curt replies didn't seem to faze her. "It sounds like becoming captain is really important to you. Will it change your life a lot?"

He nodded. "I love my job. Being captain will just take it to a higher level. I'll still be able to be out in the field with my guys and helping people, but I'll have more responsibility and..."

"More prestige?" Her brows arched.

Damn she was perceptive. "Sure. But it's just more. I'm not sure how to explain." *It's something my dad could brag about, like he brags about my brother, the entrepreneur wiz.*

When Jake was eleven years old, his mom had explained how his dad was first-generation American and had seen how hard his parents worked to provide for the family once they'd emigrated from Mexico. His grandparents had been disappointed his dad chose to go to culinary school and become a chef.

Despite the fact his dad was passionate about his work and a successful chef, Jake's grandparents viewed a college education for their children and grandchildren as the ultimate goal for starting over in a new country. After they'd passed away in a car accident when Jake and Rafe were in high school, his dad was the one to carry the "responsibility of an education" torch for them. You'd think his dad would remember how it felt.

And so, his father constantly commented on the status of his big brother's career, the wealth he'd accumulated at such a young age, and rarely discussed Jake's firefighting career. Stock market portfolio trumped saving lives and land every single time. Their roles were defined in painful detail——Rafe was the smart one and Jake was the strong one. Although Rafe was strong, despite all the shit he gave him, and Jake wasn't a slacker.

"Jake?" Amanda's eyes widened. Shit, how long

had he been ruminating about wanting daddy to be proud of him?

He snapped himself back to the present. "Sorry. I just feel called to it."

"Keep focusing on the 'why.' College is a long, difficult road and the more defined your goal is, the more you can anchor into that desire to push you to finish." Her smile was gentle. "Back to school. Let's look over your notes together, okay?"

He chewed the inside of his cheek. She was right: he'd focus on being the best man he could be.

His phone beeped. "Hold on one second. Go ahead and take a look." He slid the college bound spiral notebook over toward her and grabbed his phone.

She flipped the cover open and began thumbing through it.

He turned his attention to the screen and grimaced at the text. *Stopping by in about 15. Got take out from Chins.*

"Everything okay?" Amanda looked up from her perusal.

He worked to keep his tone neutral. "Yeah, my brother is swinging by with Chinese food."

"Now? Did he not know you had plans?" Amanda's eyebrows rose.

"He didn't ask. Sorry, he drops by all the time." Jake frowned.

"Can you tell him to come by another time or would that be rude?" She tilted her head to the side, her eyes wide.

"He'll complain because he's already almost here. He lives down in La Jolla. How do you feel about Chinese food?" Although his appetite was gone because the thought of Rafe charming Amanda made his gut churn.

"I like it, but…" She gazed down at all the school supplies covering the counter. "Does he know you're in school?"

"No. Crap. He's going to think we're on a date." He jumped to his feet and began piling the books and notebooks up. Damn it, he'd have to stuff everything into a cupboard again.

Amanda looked away from him. "We can just say I was bringing Stella over. I'm the dog mom. Definitely not a Friday night date." Her voice chilled.

The temperature in the room dropped to arctic levels. *Perfect.* "Well, when we were done I was going to see if you wanted to order in dinner anyway. I bet Rafe is bringing enough food for ten people."

"You were?" She gazed up at him, her expression impassive.

He nodded. "I was. You okay hanging out with my brother? Well, it's kind of awkward, but he'll be here any minute."

She shrugged. "Okay. Tonight I just really wanted to get a feel for how your notes are organized and make sure you've got a strict study schedule. That's what's key because until I look at your full curriculum, I'm not sure how much I can help. And it's been a while. But we can finish up after we eat, right?"

"Definitely. I'll let Rafe know you don't have much time and hurry him up." He'd boot Rafe out the minute the last bite of Kung Pao Shrimp passed his lips.

"Delivery." Rafe's deep voice called from the hallway.

Jake crossed the room and opened the door. His brother stood with two stuffed white bags and a sheepish grin on his face. "How's this for service?"

"Well, if I'd actually ordered something, pretty good."

Rafe strolled in, headed straight to the counter, and set down the bags. Mouthwatering spicy scents permeated the air. His brother halted at the granite island and stared at Amanda, then glanced back at Jake. "Oh man, I'm sorry I didn't mean to crash your date."

He flashed his killer smile at Amanda. "Hi, I'm Rafael, Jake's big brother. I didn't know he had company."

Amanda stared at his big brother for a moment, her beautiful face composed. "Oh, I'm not really company, I'm just dropping off Stella. I'm Amanda." She stood and reached a slender hand across the counter.

Rafe clasped Amanda's hand in his and his eyes narrowed. "Are you the same Amanda who tutored Jake in high school?"

"Yes, that's me, but that was a long time ago." Pink colored her high cheekbones.

"So you're sure I'm not interrupting a romantic Friday night date or anything? I mean I can leave the food for you guys." Rafe's gaze swung between the two of them, and a smile played around his lips.

She shook her head, her silky blond hair moving over her shoulders. "Nope, I'm just here for the dog."

Jake ground his molars together. Rafe was beginning to tick him off.

Amanda's blush deepened. "No romantic date. But the food smells delicious, what did you bring?"

Damn she looked stunning with her golden hair, flushed cheeks, and brilliant green eyes.

How soon could he kick his brother out of his apartment?

His brother's lips hitched as he opened the white bags. "More like what didn't I bring? Jake, grab some plates, would you? Amanda, have a seat and let the Cruz brothers serve you dinner."

Amanda laughed. "Oh don't be silly, I can serve myself."

"Our parents taught us better than that, right Jake?"

Jake nodded, but remained rooted to the spot. He wanted Amanda McNeill all to himself. He'd be having a little chat with his brother about these constant impromptu visits. Especially now Amanda might be at his apartment on a regular basis.

"Plates?" Rafe's brow creased.

Jake shifted into motion and went to the cabinet and pulled down three royal blue ceramic plates, ones his mom had given him when he'd moved out of the house. When he turned, Rafe already had opened cartons and spread them across the pale gray granite island.

He set down the dishes, grabbed some forks, and tore off three paper towels for napkins. Next time he went to the grocery store, he'd buy some real napkins. Just in case.

Amanda insisted on serving herself, managing to hide the fact her left shoulder was injured. She had barely taken enough food to feed a toddler—a few shrimps, some broccoli, and one water chestnut.

"Are you sure you like Chinese?" Jake asked.

She nodded as she speared a single shrimp. "I do, I just don't have a huge appetite. Thanks."

"So are you guys going to be filming more movies at Pacific Vista Ranch?" Rafe said.

Amanda froze, her fork halfway to her lips. "No, that movie last summer was a one-off. We'll keep the focus on the horse breeding operation. Why?" Her tutor voice had returned.

Rafe shrugged. "I work in finance and invest in a variety of projects. If you were going to be filming there regularly, I'd like the chance to invest."

"You'll just have to head to Hollywood, I guess." She popped the shrimp into her mouth and Jake struggled not to focus on her full lips.

And Rafe just kept going. "Did I hear your father is working back up in L.A.?"

"Rafe." Jake frowned and wished again that he'd ignored his brother's text and door knock for that matter. Amanda was freezing up. Couldn't his brother read her body language? Hear the chill in her voice?

"I focus on my own work. So Jake says you live in La Jolla?" She was definitely adept at avoiding topics she didn't want to discuss.

They finished up the meal with Rafe and Amanda chatting about things like the beach and the weather while Jake primarily ate in silence. The faster they finished dinner, the sooner he could be alone with Amanda again. The minute he finished eating, he stood and started clearing the food and collecting the plates.

His brother needed to take a hint and get out of there. Pronto.

An eternity later, his brother finally caught the hint and gave him a quick nod. Thank god.

Rafe rose from his seat, clasped Amanda's hand, and gazed into her eyes. What the actual hell was he doing? "It's been great meeting you Amanda. I hope I'll get to see you again soon. We're having a family picnic at the beach tomorrow. You should bring Stella and join us."

Amanda smiled at his brother. "A family picnic?"

"Not sure if Jake told you, but our dad is an incredible chef. You've got to like pico de gallo though, especially with lots of jalapenos."

She gazed between his brother and him, "You didn't tell me your dad was a chef. What's his specialty?"

Why was Amanda still holding Rafe's hand?

Jake wanted her smiles directed at him, but stood there watching, unable to do anything about what was now definitely flirting.

"Our dad's from Ensenada, so he makes a lot of seafood. He'll usually make fish tacos on the beach. Come. They'd get a kick out of Stella." Rafe's gaze was locked on Amanda like a shark about to gobble up a snack.

"Maybe I will." Amanda smiled up at Rafe.

What the hell? About ten hours later, Rafe released her hand. Good thing because Jake was beginning to think tackling his brother and tossing him out the door was a great idea.

This evening was not going as he'd planned. Granted, he'd decided he couldn't date her and mix up business with pleasure, but he'd be damned if his brother went out with her. And from the feral gleam in Rafe's dark eyes, his brother would definitely like to have Amanda as another one of his conquests. Damn it.

*Not on my watch.*

After Rafe left, Jake finished clearing away the cartons and put the dishes in the dishwasher. When Amanda tried to help him clean up, he insisted he would do it. If she weren't going to look out for her injury, he'd have to do it for her. Although he'd like to do more than just protect her. *School. Captain. Priorities. Focus.*

"Should we start over? Where are the books?" Amanda watched him from her perch on the barstool.

He hurried over to the cabinet where he'd

shoved the books and returned to the island. He spread the books and notebook out on the countertop.

"Great, I'll just get started and finish reviewing what you've got. Then I'll write out some suggestions." She smiled up at him and he swallowed over his now dry throat.

"Can I get you a drink?"

"Sure, I'll have a glass of the pinot grigio I brought over." She gazed up through her fan of dark lashes.

Those cat eyes punched him in the gut every time he looked at her. He headed to the refrigerator and resisted sticking his head into it to cool off. "I'll pour you a glass."

Jake poured her some white wine and poured himself some water. He needed to remain clear-headed tonight. For his studies and more importantly right now, for his self-control around her. When his brother had been flirting with her, he'd felt the jealousy surge through him.

She accepted the glass and the same familiar jolt shot through his fingertips when they brushed hers. "So your brother seems nice. Are you two close?"

Jake joined her at the counter. Amanda thought Rafe was nice? "Sure, we're close. I mean we're just different, but he's cool."

"My sisters and I are all really different too, but that's what makes it interesting, right?" She sipped her wine.

He considered. He'd never really thought of it

that way. "Sure."

She looked like she was going to dig further and then pressed her pink lips together.

His brother and Amanda had way more in common than Jake did with her. They were both the same age, both had genius IQs, degrees from impressive universities, cleverness, and wealth. All he could offer her was his body and his heart.

His *heart?* He choked on a sip of water. Man, he needed to pull it together. They could be friends. They could be co-parents of Stella. They could work out together. But he sure as hell couldn't offer her his heart.

He knew his brain and it could only operate on one goal at a time. Being fire captain was the most important dream of his life. Or at least it had been until he'd seen her again.

He slammed the heart compartment shut. Fire captain. Make his parents proud. Exceed everyone's expectations. That's what mattered, no matter how incredible Amanda was. And it wasn't like she was guaranteed to reciprocate his feelings.

No, a prestigious career was tangible. Objective. And not beyond his reach.

"You okay?"

He nodded. He forced himself to soften his grip on his glass before he shattered it. He was fine.

# CHAPTER 10

AMANDA SHIFTED ON THE STOOL and prayed for inspiration. Jake's broad shoulders were rigid. His stoic façade was showing a crack or two. But the attraction between them was undeniable. His heated gaze on her when he didn't think she noticed, the warmth of his long square hands when he'd brushed against her, and his adoration for Stella all sent electricity skittering up her spine. Not to mention he'd admitted to his teenaged crush on her. Was he jealous of his brother's flirting with her? She smiled to herself. *Good*.

Not that Rafe wasn't a gorgeous and obviously successful guy, but she'd felt no spark. She also recognized a charming player when she met one and no, thank you very much. When he kept pressing her about movies and her father's potential Hollywood renaissance, she'd had to dig her fingernails into her palms to remain calm. Her temper was nothing like her dad's and sisters', but when provoked, she definitely showed her McNeill blood. Discussing the Hollywood lifestyle wasn't an option.

Last summer, the protective bubble of life on

Pacific Vista Ranch had been pricked and finished forever. Whether the McNeills were ready or not. Now she was finally ready to make changes, and if she had her way, Jake would be a part of her new improved life.

The dog he rescued definitely was and darn it, she wanted the man too. Something about Jake drew her in and not just his mouthwatering muscles and sweet heart. She gulped more of the crisp, cold wine.

What was going on behind that gorgeous olive skin and obsidian eyes? He was an enigma and one her analytical brain wanted to figure out. Well, her brain wasn't the only part of her interested in him. The more she pondered, the more certain she felt he'd invited her over for tutoring to dip his toe in the water. To be safe.

She'd spent most of her life always choosing the safe path. She'd been the big sister to her twin siblings when they'd lost their mom. The shy, private bookworm, her books and her animals had always comforted her. She was the only McNeill family member who didn't either wear their heart on their sleeve or have a temper like a rollercoaster.

No matter how much she despised the label, she was a practical woman. Sensible even. When Jake and she were together, undeniable chemistry sizzled in the air between them.

As a practical woman, the smart move would be to take the situation into her own hands. She'd test it out to see how he reacted, but if he was even half as attracted to her as she was to him, she'd make the first move.

It was the sensible thing to do, considering the circumstances.

What did she have to lose?

Well, besides her pride and possibly her free personal trainer.

And her dog.

But what if her gamble paid off? She shivered.

He sat quietly next to her, the warmth from his skin reaching across the space between them. There was just so much smooth bronzed skin, stretched taut against all the sinewy muscles. She'd never been this close to such a perfect physical specimen.

Heat pooled low in her belly. This was ridiculous. They hadn't even kissed yet and she was on fire for him. She'd never had this type of reaction to a guy before. Maybe if she had, she would have gone on more dates over the last six years.

And maybe because she hadn't gone on many dates over the last six years was exactly why she was so on fire. Regardless.

She huffed out a breath and squared her shoulders. Tutor first. Pounce later. "Well, your notes look like you've organized them well, but that didn't help you on this first test. I think you should copy the notes onto index cards, kind of like flash cards, and test yourself that way. It will help hammer in the points and the cards give you the information in manageable chunks. What do you think?"

She looked at him over the rim of her glass and

took a sip of wine. His gaze was fastened on her mouth and she could swear it tracked the liquid down her throat as she swallowed. Amanda's pulse began to thrum. Oh yes, he was as aware of her as she was of him. The thrum turned into a hammering. Could he hear it?

He continued to stare at her for what seemed like forever. "I'll try anything."

*Oh, I could think of many things for you to try.* Amanda shifted in her seat. Was it hot in the apartment tonight? Why had she worn a turtle-neck again? At least it had a zipper. She looked down at her notes, her mind blank. What was she saying again? Notecards. Yes.

"Good. Also, maybe once you've done that with the topic, I could test you each week and we could see? Are there practice tests available prior to the actual online one?"

He nodded. "Yeah, they have a few samples. I think for every topic."

"Well, you could take the sample tests and then we could review them. You can track where you were having trouble. If you can pinpoint whether it's the time parameters, the subject matter, or the written-to-audio format, we can address it. How did you handle your tests for the fire academy?" She fired the questions at him, eager to move on to the next stage of their evening.

Jake kept his gaze focused on the computer and shared how he'd been able to pass all the stringent requirements for paramedic school. Would he look up at her again?

He lifted those deep penetrating eyes to meet her gaze and she almost melted on the spot. Good lord. She needed a fan at this rate or she'd implode on his bar stool.

"I talk to my advisor next week and need to make sure they'll give me another chance. But then yeah, I'll try the cards and the sample tests." He shifted on his stool, reaching to pull the laptop away from the center of the counter. His ripped forearms rested on the granite, just begging for attention. Begging to be touched.

"Great, sounds like a plan." Before she could stop herself, her hand shot out and landed on his arm. Her hand looked practically ghostly against his dark skin. The silky texture of his skin and the crisp roughness of his hair sent a shot of heat through her entire body.

Jake jolted, but didn't pull away. She stroked from his strong wrist along his muscular forearm. His eyes were black now; she couldn't discern where his pupils began and his irises ended. She leaned in closer and his clean masculine scent enveloped her. Her gaze dropped to his parted lips.

Now or never. She brushed her mouth against his, and he remained frozen. *Oh no.*

Mortified, she pulled back. Before she could create any distance, his large hand reached up and cupped her chin and the warmth from his long fingers singed her skin. Their gazes locked. With his other hand, he cupped her jaw, and slid his fingers into her silky hair. She remained motionless, unable to look away. He lowered his sculpted lips to hers, and a moan escaped her at the delicious taste of him. Her arms wrapped around his back and the length of her pressed against him.

Both his hands were on her, skimming up her jaw to hold her head still while he plundered her mouth. His tongue tangled with hers, her mind blanked, and sensation flooded through her. Sparks flitted along her skin, her face was on fire, and heat coursed through her veins. Her arms slid around his neck and she dug her fingers into his thick, ebony hair.

This. This was what she'd been missing. She scooted in closer, wanting him to take the kiss even deeper, wanting…

Jake jumped back so fast his stool crashed behind him. Stella erupted into a flurry of barking and scurried away from them, her nails clacking on the hardwood floors. Suddenly a chill shot through her.

*Oh no.* Oh god, had she just messed things up? All the fire threatening to erupt inside her died out. Amanda bit the inside of her cheek. "I'm sorry, I didn't…"

What could she say? I fell against your mouth? Could she curl up and die under the barstool now?

Jake practically ran over to Stella, who was now cowering against the wall. "It's okay, sweet girl. I'm sorry." He stroked the dog's head and she seemed to relax.

Although she hated to see Stella spooked, Amanda welcomed the distraction. She hurried over to them. "She's shaking. She obviously has dealt with some trauma, maybe she was yelled at. Or worse."

She crouched down next to Jake, careful not to touch him after whatever *that* had been. The dog quieted when she laid her hands on Stella's side. They remained that way, soothing and petting the dog for a few minutes. Then, Stella popped up to her feet and trotted back over to her bed. Crisis averted. At least the dog's crisis.

Jake stood, headed to the refrigerator, and refilled his water glass. Was it her imagination or was the back of his neck bright red?

"She seems okay now. Is that it for tonight?" He turned to look at her but his gaze focused just over her shoulder, not meeting hers.

She'd returned to the breakfast bar and swallowed another sip of wine, liquid courage and all that, and responded in what she hoped was her cool, calm, and collected voice. Pretend like nothing had happened, just like he was doing. "Well, I think so. Just let me know when the next exam is so I can help you prep and then review the sample test before."

"Yeah, that would be great." He stayed in the kitchen and an awkward silence fell over the room.

Time to go. She slid on her serene face, praying her embarrassment didn't show. How could she have read him so wrong? Now she knew why she'd never tried to make the first move before. She rose and looked around for her purse. Plenty of time to berate herself in the privacy of her car ride home.

Stella rubbed against her legs. "You stay here for the next few days, girl." Amanda scratched the mutt's ears and leaned down to give her a smooch.

Jake finally approached, but maintained several feet between them. She gazed down, her hair sliding forward, shrouding her face from his gaze. It wasn't like he hadn't kissed her back. Deepened their embrace really. Geez, was he afraid she was going to pounce on him or something? Her embarrassment morphed into mild insult. He'd been the one with the crush on her after all.

"Thanks for everything tonight." Monosyllable man was back in town.

"You're welcome. Let me know once you've spoken to your advisor and we'll go from there." No way was she bringing up the personal training right now.

"Will do." He sounded like a damn robot.

Her back went ramrod straight. "Well, I'll see you later." When he didn't budge, she crossed the space to the door and opened it.

"Later."

Amanda cringed and closed the door behind her. Maybe he was really shy––her instincts couldn't have been completely wrong. His passionate kiss hadn't been her imagination. She wasn't finished with Jake McNeill yet. Not even close.

# CHAPTER 11

"**W**HOA. DID YOU STAY UP all night?" Samantha McNeill Ericsson demanded before Amanda even had a chance to inhale her first sip of pitch-black coffee, strong enough to walk on its own.

She took three deep cleansing breaths and narrowed her eyes at her younger sister across the breakfast nook's large table. "Are you saying I look like death warmed over?"

Sam immediately looked contrite. "I'm sorry. You're always my beautiful big sister, but you're pasty white and have circles under your eyes. I know it can be tough to sleep with a shoulder injury and I'm just worried about you."

Amanda sighed. Sam's bark was always worse than her bite. And her bark had softened considerably since Holt Ericsson had shown up on their ranch last year. The two had despised each other on sight, but over the period of time he participated in the movie filming on the ranch, their dislike morphed into passionate love. And now they were married and Sam was happier than Amanda had ever seen her. She was thrilled her sister had found love.

What would it be like to bask in the passion and commitment Sam and Holt shared? At this point, she didn't need the commitment part, but a satisfying fling with one hot young fireman sounded pretty appealing.

"It's really not that bad. Thank god it's my left side and not my right." Amanda sighed. "I've just got a lot on my mind." She'd tossed and turned all night. Not because of the nagging pain in her shoulder. Nope, because the scene of her kissing Jake before he leapt away from her like he'd been sprayed with a fire hose ran on a non-stop replay loop in her weary brain.

She swigged the rest of the coffee and went to pour herself another cup. She might as well mainline it because she was wiped out.

"Anything to do with the hot firefighter and the rescued pup?" Sam waggled her dark eyebrows.

"Yes, that's part of it." Her responsible, predictable existence was evaporating before her eyes and now she was questioning all her choices. The only choice which seemed clear was seducing Jake. A fun affair with him could jumpstart the rest of her new life. If only she could convince him they could enjoy each other without compromising their current bargain.

"Oooh, really? I haven't met him yet but Dylan said he looks like the guy from the stripper movie. What's the problem?"

Amanda's lips twitched. "Dylan's right. We should just call him Magic Jake. Remember the guy from last year's fire, when we were evacuating the horses? The one who wouldn't look at me and talked to you?"

Sam nodded. "Yeah, that was so weird."

"Well, that's him. And, turns out I tutored him in high school. But I thought he was interested in dating me and I was mistaken." Although he had kissed her for a few beautiful passionate seconds before he'd retreated.

Sam sat back in her seat, flipping her long auburn braid over her opposite shoulder. "How is that possible? Are you sure?"

Amanda grimaced. "No mistaking it. When he came to walk Stella, I thought he was asking me on a date, but he didn't. So now he's going to be my personal trainer for a while. I'm going to try to change his mind."

"Hmmm…maybe he didn't realize you liked him that way? I mean, you're kind of the ice princess––maybe he's just intimidated?" Sam reached across the table and clasped her hand.

"Oh he knew. And please don't call me that." Ice princess. Amanda hated the nickname some boys had given her in high school once they'd moved from L.A. Learning to rein in her emotions and assume a composed facade after her mom's death and the ensuing nightmare had been her coping mechanism. Otherwise, she'd probably have lost her marbles.

"I'm sorry. But I'm serious. Maybe he's intimidated, especially if you used to be his tutor. Wait, was he the skinny little boy who gave you flowers?"

Amanda nodded, her lips hitching up at the corners. "Yeah, like I told Dylan, he's put on about one hundred pounds of muscle since high school."

"That's so cute. It's like a 1980s romcom." Sam grinned.

"You know, you and Dylan's twin brains are disturbing at times. She made the same comment." Amanda shrugged one shoulder. "But I don't want to discuss it. We're meeting Leo soon, right? What's the plan?"

Sam leaned back against the seat cushions. "Well, breeding season is about to kick into high gear and you know how stressful it gets. I was thinking we bring on Leo to help me with all the breeding and foaling. You could focus on the lab work, prepping and shipping the doses, the paperwork…"

Amanda wrinkled her nose. "Yeah, yeah, all the technical stuff and none of the fun stuff. You know how much I love foaling." Much as she hated to admit it, her sister was right. No way could she do any of the physically demanding tasks right now.

"I know. It doesn't mean you can't be there during the foaling, right? So how long is recovery?" Sam smiled at her.

Amanda nodded. "True. PT is four to six weeks. I'm going to be a good girl and do all my PT and also work with Jake to build up my overall strength."

"Oh, that'll be fun to get all sweaty and breathless with him. And maybe even grow some muscles, twiggy." Sam smirked.

Amanda dropped her head back on the seat rest and closed her eyes. "Sam. I'm questioning what I'm even doing as an equine vet."

Sam gasped. "What? You're amazing with the horses. You can't let one freak accident throw your confidence. I was only joking calling you twiggy."

"Sam, I totally ignored Cowgirl's obvious signs. I'm lucky my injuries aren't more severe. I don't know. After this last year, I'm just starting to question everything I'm doing, you know?" She opened her eyes and sat up.

Sam leaned forward again. "I do know. But what do you mean everything?"

"Sam, all I've done is live here, go to school, and be the resident vet. I've never traveled like Dylan, or been a groundbreaker like you. I'm thirty years old and have never done anything else." Amanda exhaled an unsteady breath and stared down at her clasped hands.

Sam reached over and massaged her good shoulder. "Whoa. Amanda. I had no idea you felt that way. You've always seemed so confident and certain. What do you want to do?"

Amanda threw her hands up in the air. "That's the thing. I've got no clue. Don't get me wrong. I love my job and the ranch. But is there something else for me? Stella has gotten me thinking about working with small animals again. Like what I thought I'd do before we lost Mom and Dad bought the ranch."

Sam's brown eyes rounded like saucers. "You've never mentioned anything—"

"I don't think I realized until you and Holt got married. Now, Dad's returning to some film work and I'm just good old reliable Amanda. And maybe I want to change."

"Do you mean you'd want me to ask Leo if he wants your job and you go look for something else?" Sam whispered.

Amanda's gut clenched. "Hey, not so fast. I'm not giving up my job. I'm just trying to articulate what I'm feeling."

"Okay. Well, you've got some time to reflect while you're recovering. But I know a great way for you to blow off some steam and clear your mind." Samantha grinned. "Magic Jake."

"Magic Jake didn't ask me out, but we are getting together soon to work out." Amanda tapped her index finger against her lips.

"Wear some cute yoga pants, make sure he gives you some hands-on adjustments, and take charge. He loved when you bossed him around once upon a time." Sam's grin grew wicked.

Amanda laughed. "You're too funny. But maybe you're right."

"Aren't I always?" Sam lounged back against the seat cushions. "That's settled, but Leo should be here soon. Do you agree we ask him to handle the breeding and foaling and you handle the rest?"

Amanda pursed her lips. She really didn't want anyone handling her duties in her vet clinic and barns, but what choice did she have? "Fine. When does he get here?"

Sam glanced up at the clock over the enormous six-burner stove. "In about twenty minutes. I told him to come to the house, cool?"

Amanda rose. "Let me go change clothes and I'll be back down. Don't start without me." She crossed the room and headed back to her bed-room.

"I'm happy to help and would really love to be a part of Pacific Vista Ranch full-time." Dr. Leo Dunmore smiled across the kitchen table at Amanda and Sam.

Amanda stiffened. Had his smile always reminded her of a toothy cartoon shark or was it just today?

Sam laid one hand on Amanda's leg under the table and squeezed. "Leo, we really appreciate your enthusiasm and I know you'll do a great job filling in for Amanda for a little while."

The vet nodded enthusiastically, his dark, curly brown hair bouncing around his round head. "Who knows how long Amanda will be out though, right? What if your shoulder injury is worse than they think and you can't do any of the physical duties anymore?"

Amanda ground her teeth and dug deep for her usual cool, which come to think of it wasn't in rampant supply these days. "Thanks for your concern, but I'm sure I'll be fine sooner than later. Any reason you're so eager to work here full-time?

Is there a problem at the other ranches where you work?"

Dunmore worked for a few different horse farms around Bonsall and Murietta, in addition to Rancho Santa Fe. He had a great reputation and had come to help out on a few occasions and they'd always been happy with his work. Right now, however, his over-eager attitude and apparent desire for her permanent retirement was ticking her off.

He focused his watery blue eyes on her and smiled again. "No, it's all great. It's just Pacific Vista Ranch is the ultimate, you know? Or maybe you don't realize it because it's yours. You guys have the ultimate operation here, Hercules is one of the top stallions in the country, who wouldn't want to be here full-time?"

"Apparently you think I don't." She couldn't keep the chill out of her voice. Of course she appreciated what they'd built.

Sam squeezed her leg again and Amanda almost laughed. Talk about a role reversal. Usually, she was the one trying to keep Sam's hair-trigger temper under control and act as the neutral party in every situation. Yes, things definitely had changed.

Leo sat back with a frown. Ah, finally cluing in to how he might be coming across. "Oh gosh, Amanda, that's not it at all. I apologize if I'm over-eager. I'm just really excited to work here."

Amanda's shoulders relaxed. Lack of sleep, a new pattern of embarrassing herself regularly, and this accident were not doing her personality any favors. "It's fine. Well, when can you start?"

"I'm here today if you need me and I'm free about twenty hours a week, but starting next month I could be available up to forty or fifty if necessary."

Amanda bit back a protest. The horses had to come first. Her pride could take a back seat, where it belonged. Heck, at this rate, her pride should just tie itself to the back bumper, like those noisy tin cans and streamers on a "just married" car. Clanking along in the rearview mirror.

"Today would be excellent. Why don't we go down to the barn first, and then over to the clinic to get you oriented. Sound good?" Sam pushed to her feet.

"Works for me. Amanda?" Leo stood.

He wasn't a tall man, or particularly muscular. In fact, he probably only had about twenty pounds on her. She reminded herself she didn't need to be some big bruiser to be an effective equine vet. They had grooms to assist. She'd done a damn good job for the last six years and needed to stop questioning herself. Her injury was just an isolated mistake, not a negation to her entire career.

"You two head on down to the barn. I'll be there in a few minutes." Her phone had pinged, but she hadn't wanted to check the message in front of her sister and the other vet. Just in case.

Just in case it was Jake.

"Take your time. We'll be down there a while." Sam smiled and left with Leo.

Amanda grabbed her phone from her purse and sure enough, a text from Jake was waiting for her. She drew in a deep inhale and held it for four counts, and exhaled for eight. She needed to make sure her nervous system didn't go haywire before she read his message. She tapped on the phone screen.

*Good morning. Stella asked if you'd meet us at Cardiff State Beach? Family picnic & my dad's famous fish tacos.*

Amanda's belly performed a long slow roll. Meet Jake's family? Maybe she hadn't scared him away last night by kissing him after all. Maybe he'd tossed and turned too and wanted her just as much as she wanted him.

She smiled down at her phone. *I'm doing some work now, when?*

*We're heading down @3.*

Although emotion wasn't usually discernable through text messages, Jake was acting like nothing had happened last night. The more time she spent with him the better. New life. New chances. And if she were assuming incorrectly, she'd still get to see Stella frolicking in the ocean.

*Sure. Where will you be?*

His response popped up immediately. *Right by the main parking lot. Text me and we'll meet you.*

Amanda's lips hitched up. Maybe she had imagined him jumping away from her last night after all.

*See you then. Can I bring anything?*

*Just you.*

Excitement shimmered through her veins. Work first. Fun later.

Perhaps her gamble had paid off after all.

# CHAPTER 12

JAKE STOOD WITH THE COOL surf swirling around his ankles and the kiss of the Pacific breeze ruffling his hair. Although he was the king of compartmentalizing, he couldn't erase visions of last night. He'd spent one long, sweaty night, despite the two freezing cold showers, reliving the moment Amanda had leaned in and pressed her full, beautiful mouth to his. He'd dreamed of that moment from the time he was fifteen years old, it came, and what did he do when fantasy became reality?

Kissed her back, freaked out, and capsized the barstool like a clumsy oaf. He rolled his eyes. Amanda wasn't the first woman to initiate a kiss, but she was the first woman who gave him heart palpitations. Maybe he shouldn't try so hard to keep her at arm's length. She'd kissed him first, so obviously she didn't see an issue with them being involved beyond tutoring. Was he being over the top with drawing such a hard line rule?

But he could barely control himself around her. All he wanted to do was look at her, listen to her, touch her…He already had a tough enough time focusing on school and studying. How could he succeed if he allowed himself to do anything else? He'd had to run away because he just couldn't risk it. His gut told him pretty damn clearly that if they got involved, he'd not be able to concentrate on school. He'd concentrate on her.

Until he spoke with his advisor, he wouldn't know if he'd be able to stay in the program. So, he'd have to resist the one woman he'd dreamed about for almost half his life. Not like he could tell her to wait four years for him to graduate. They weren't in high school anymore.

Stella yanked on the leash on her perpetual fruitless quest to catch get one of the seagulls taunting her nearby. "Sorry, girl, keep on dreaming." He laughed at Stella's quizzical expression.

His phone buzzed. *Just parked. Where are you?*

*Meet me by the lifeguard tower.* His heartbeat accelerated. He strode across the sand, Stella trotting along beside him, her tail wagging like a propeller. It was probably a toss-up between which one of them was more excited to see Amanda.

She stood wearing jeans rolled up at the ankles, a soft fuzzy aqua hoodie, and flip-flops. Her blonde hair was bundled into one of those messy braids and rested over one slender shoulder. Would she like it if he tugged it tight and pulled her head back to kiss her? He exhaled. She was meeting his family for a picnic, not exactly the right time to make out.

Amanda caught sight of he and Stella and waved and started forward. Stella saw her and bolted toward her. And wasn't she lucky to not have to hide her enthusiasm?

After Amanda kissed him last night, he wasn't sure he'd be able to hide his attraction to her. He wouldn't have actually invited her today because it was a hell of a lot smarter to have some space between them, but his brother had gone ahead and done it for him. And told his parents about her and the dog.

They'd insisted he invite her—even just to thank her for saving Stella. Now his parents probably thought Rafe wanted to date her and for all he knew, Rafe did want to date her.

Over his dead body. He might not be able to have Amanda, but he'd be damned if his brother moved in on her.

"Gotta love San Diego in February, right?" She crouched down and hugged the dog, who he could have sworn moaned in ecstasy. Lucky dog.

The weather. He could talk about the weather. "Right? Sixty-eight and sunny. Do you get out to the beach much?"

"You'd think so, living less than ten miles away, right? But I've spent most of my time on the ranch. So thanks for helping me out of my rut." She stood, keeping one hand on Stella's head and gazed out toward the Pacific's crashing indigo waves.

Out of the corner of his eye, he saw Rafe waving at them. Time to suck it up and introduce Amanda to his family. Every muscle in his body tightened up in anticipation of Rafe hitting on her again and his parents interrogating her. He would protect her if they got too familiar.

"Let's head over. My dad's been grilling halibut for tacos." Act normal. One foot in front of the other.

Rafe jogged up to meet them and enveloped Amanda in a hug. "Hey, stranger, so glad you could make it. My parents are dying to meet the woman who saved Stella and convinced their son to take care of her." He flashed his white teeth.

Jake squeezed Stella's leash so hard the fabric was in danger of disintegrating. Hugging her? What the actual hell? He'd met her once.

Amanda stood stiffly, without returning the hug. With a polite smile, she stepped back toward Jake. "Nice to see you."

Jake grinned and resisted pumping his hands in the air. Yeah, she didn't want his brother. She'd kissed *him* after all. She was *his*. And he needed to get a grip.

Rafe appeared unphased and kept the smile pasted on. "Dad and Mom are brandishing cervezas and tortilla chips, so come on over."

They followed Rafe across the surprisingly full beach, the sand powdery soft between his bare toes. Even in late February, the locals enjoyed hanging out and savoring the natural beauty of North County San Diego. There weren't many tourists this time of year.

Nobody spoke for a moment and Jake wondered what Amanda was thinking of it all. When he snuck a glance at her, her expression gave nothing away. Her poker face rivaled his. Hopefully the afternoon with his family would be simple and fun. If Rafe embarrassed him, he'd be a dead man.

Amanda's nerves were strung tight and she worked to relax her jaw. If she clenched it any tighter, she'd probably crack a few molars. This whole situation was beyond uncomfortable. Maybe if Jake hadn't freaked out when they kissed last night she wouldn't feel so uncomfortable. But he had. She couldn't read him today, but he had the stoic shy guy down. Like she could ask him about it anyway. *So, umm, why did you almost do a back flip to get away from me after we kissed? Was it my breath?*

Awkward. Awkward. Awkward. If he'd kissed her back for more than thirty seconds and they'd decided to see where their ridiculous chemistry could take them, it would be one thing. Jake's posture was natural, although the death grip on Stella's leash gave away his tension. Rafe just flitted along without a care in the world.

More problematic was Rafe's enthusiastic greeting along with the fact he'd engineered this whole day. She couldn't tell if he wanted to date her, if he was trying to push she and Jake together, or what. Maybe the Cruzes were a close-knit family and got together regularly and it meant nothing.

A curvy woman with wavy chestnut hair and a San Diego Padres sweatshirt smiled and waved at her. "You must be Amanda, the tutor veterinarian."

Amanda froze. The tutor veterinarian? Oh crap, how did she know she was tutoring Jake? She whipped her head to the side and caught his gaze. How was she supposed to respond to that? "Hi, I'm Amanda McNeill."

Jake was glaring at Rafe. But his brother didn't know about his decision to seek a college degree, did he? Odd.

"I'm Lisa and this is my husband, Eduardo." She gestured to the tall, olive-skinned man next to her, who held two chilled plastic glasses in his large hands.

He handed a beer to her first and one to Jake. "Nice to meet you, Amanda. Hope you like Modelo and jalapenos."

"Thanks. Hopefully not together." She smiled politely. Okay, she could handle a family picnic. Diplomacy was in her DNA.

"Rafe tells me you're a doctor. That's quite impressive for one so young." Eduardo gazed intently at her.

Amanda felt a quiver of embarrassment. Oh my goodness, he was leading with the doctor part. "I am. I'm thirty and I wanted to be a vet since I was a kid, kind of like Jake wanted to be a firefighter."

Eduardo smiled. "Yes, Jake was always rescuing animals when he was a kid. We're proud of how strong and brave he is. You know Rafe's got his MBA, right? You two have the big brains in this group."

Amanda's brows drew together. What kind of

comment was that? She squared her shoulders. "I've never thought that degrees were the measure of intelligence. There are plenty of people with advanced degrees who aren't that bright, they just know how to work hard, and then there are plenty of brilliant people that school doesn't work well for."

"Of course, of course." He nodded. "It's just in our family, Rafe was the first one to go to college, not to mention graduate school. We're very proud of his achievements."

Amanda forced herself to relax. Why had that sounded like a dig on Jake? Out of the side of her eye, she saw him take a swig of beer, and stare down at the dog.

She nodded. "I'm sure you are. But paramedic school and firefighting are incredibly competitive too. My family is all over the board. My sister Dylan is an artist and went to art school. She's a genius and college would have been a waste of her talent. One of my stepbrothers also chose a different route. I'm just saying that a piece of paper doesn't actually impart any true measure of success."

"But weren't you a tutor in school? And vet school is more competitive than medical school, isn't it?" Lisa asked, her voice gentle.

"Yes, I was. And yes, it is." How in the world were they having such a serious and personal discussion when they were at the beach for tacos and beer? Time to change the subject.

Rafe swooped in and saved the day. "Stop

interrogating the poor woman. We have more important things to do, like you guys paying attention to your grand-dog Stella and Amanda getting to try our dad's unbelievable cooking."

Amanda smiled. Thank goodness. "Absolutely. Jake and Rafe both mentioned you're a great chef. And isn't Stella adorable?"

Stella grinned, one butterscotch ear flopping forward and the other standing straight up. If you didn't see the patches of missing fur and scabbing along her side, you'd never know she'd been a hit-and-run victim recently.

Lisa crouched down. "Come to grandma." Stella trotted over, tail wagging, more than happy to receive more love and affection.

Amanda swallowed a sip of beer and glanced off toward the ocean. More awkwardness. If she and Jake didn't see each other after their arrangement ended, she'd probably keep Stella and never see Jake again. No need to predict the future right now. She'd just try to enjoy the afternoon and see how it went.

"So if your husband is the chef, does that mean he cooks for you every day?" Amanda addressed Jake's mom.

Lisa laughed and stood. "I wish. Don't get me wrong, he cooks a lot, but when he doesn't, I'm stuck. The kitchen isn't exactly my comfort zone. Do you cook?"

Amanda shrugged one shoulder. "Well, that's debatable. My stepmom is an amazing chef too, so she's spoiled us. I'm not a foodie like the rest of my family, so I can live off toast if I have to."

Lisa looked over her shoulder at where Eduardo was at the grill with Rafe and Jake. She whispered conspiratorially, "Don't tell the Cruz men, but I could too."

Amanda's nerves began to settle. Jake's mom seemed pleasant. She wasn't so sure about his dad. Maybe she was overreacting, but his dad seemed to favor Rafe over Jake. Or maybe she was infatuated with Jake and didn't want to hear any criticism of him, implied or otherwise. Or maybe a bit of both.

"Come on over ladies, it's taco time." Eduardo called.

She and Lisa walked over to the grill, where they'd set up a small portable picnic table with everything from jalapenos, cheese, chopped tomatoes, cabbage, three types of salsa, guacamole, and sliced avocadoes. Amanda might not have a huge appetite, but she drooled looking at the colorful spread.

"Wow, you weren't kidding about doing the tacos right." Amanda said.

Rafe grinned. "Wait until you taste one. There are corn and flour tortillas on the grill, which do you prefer?"

"I'll have flour, thanks. Can I do anything to help?"

Eduardo shook his head. "Don't you dare. You're our guest this afternoon. But I don't let anyone touch my grill anyway." He handed her a plate with fragrant grilled halibut heaped onto a crispy tortilla.

Once everyone was served, they sat around colorful beach chairs and dug into the feast.

Amanda groaned when she took a bite of her taco. The tender firm white fish exploded with flavor, perfectly complementing the avocado and mild salsa she'd piled on.

Jake sat up straighter in his chair next to her. "You like it?" His voice was hoarse.

She licked her lips. "It's absolutely delicious. My stepmom would love to learn how to grill fish that tastes like this. Do you ever share your secrets?" She addressed Eduardo. It was safer than looking at Jake right now. Not when he sounded so raspy and sexy.

"Only for family." Jake's dad smirked. "I do have two sons."

Jake jolted again in his chair next to her.

Heat rose in Amanda's cheeks. Oh good grief. Seriously, was Jake's dad suggesting she marry one of his sons? She'd recently discovered she wanted to sleep with Jake, but marriage wasn't in the cards anytime soon.

"Eduardo." Lisa's voice was stern. "You're embarrassing Amanda. Stop it and eat your taco."

Amanda held up her hands. "Please. You all are being silly." More like obnoxious, but she would be polite if it killed her.

Rafe simply winked at her and Jake growled under his breath. So maybe he was jealous and wasn't so immune to her after all. They ate in silence for a few minutes and she forced herself to simply enjoy the food.

"I've forgotten how the food always tastes better at the beach. Thanks again for including me." And how soon would be too soon to beat a hasty exit?

"Thanks for coming. Do you want to take Stella for a walk?" Jake asked. Stella leapt up at the mention of her name.

Amanda nodded. "Absolutely. And then I'll need to head home."

They both stood and placed their plates into the trash bag next to the small portable grill.

Eduardo, Lisa, and Rafe all stood.

"Thanks so much for coming down and thanks for taking such good care of this sweet dog. I know how much Jake loves animals and it's easy to see he's already in love." Lisa said.

Eduardo was looking between her and Jake, his eyes questioning. "Nice to meet you, Amanda. Hope to see you again." Eduardo was all manners now.

"See you soon." Rafe gave a half wave. He was also smiling, but his eyes were shadowed.

"Thanks again." Jake grabbed Stella's leash and they strolled down toward where the winter waves were breaking onto the shore.

She paused to remove her shoes, savoring the silkiness of the sand between her toes. Stella strained against the leash and Amanda reached up to comfort her. Her fingers brushed Jake's and once again heat shot up her arm to flood her entire body. Just from a light touch. How could he ignore it?

Once they'd reached the packed sand, they headed south toward Solana Beach. Amanda loved this stretch of beach where the charming little town of Cardiff-by-the-Sea turned into Solana Beach, yet another charming little town. The coastline of North County San Diego was dotted with these small communities, each with its own unique flavor.

Why didn't she come down to the beach more often? The salty breeze stroking through her hair, the chilly water washing over her feet, and the purity of the horizon where the azure blue sky met the mysterious midnight of the sea were pure magic. No more hiding out on the ranch and missing out on everything North County San Diego had to offer. Not with this beautiful locale close by.

The tension in her shoulders unfurled with each step they took away from Jake's family. Stella trotted along, yanking on the leash each time a bird flew by.

"The eternal optimist here thinks these birds will allow her to catch them." She laughed, a lightness and simple sense of joy filling her.

Jake gazed down at her and grinned. "Right? Before you got here she almost dislocated my shoulder." He paused. "Sorry, bad choice of words."

She rolled her eyes. "Oh don't worry about it. I'm not that sensitive." Right now her shoulder didn't even hurt. Much.

He smiled at her, his dark eyes crinkling at the corners. "We should take her down to Del Mar Dog Beach, where she can run around off-leash."

"That's a great idea. Our dog Kola used to love Dog Beach. I think Stella might be a swimmer. But I want her abrasions to heal up a little more. Although salt water is healing." It certainly felt healing on her feet. All the stress that had built up from the awkward time with Jake's family was washing away with the tide.

"I've always loved the beach." Jake said.

"Me too."

They walked along in comfortable silence. Amanda treasured the moments when she didn't feel like she had to fill space with words. All they had to do was enjoy the environment and the moment. One more quality they shared. What a relief.

"So, I'm sorry about my dad. He means well."

Amanda gazed up at Jake. Damn, his profile was an illustration of strength and beauty. "Oh, don't apologize." Although his dad had really seemed to favor his eldest son.

Jake halted and Stella turned her attention to dunking her head in the water and shaking it out. What a goof. "I'm serious. I don't know where he got off with all that stuff." He frowned.

"Can I be honest?"

"Why wouldn't you be?" One black brow arched.

"Well, I found it really odd. I've never had someone hammer on my education so much." She shook her head.

They continued walking and Jake appeared to be gathering his thoughts.

"My dad's parents emigrated when he was a little boy. They worked in the strawberry fields and anywhere else they could to provide a better life for my dad and his brothers. Education and opportunity were the biggest deal. My learning issues were always a disappointment to my grand-parents and to my dad."

Amanda's heart cracked. "I'm so sorry to hear that. That must have been really hard."

Jake nodded, but didn't respond.

"So you turned into the physical one and Rafe was cast as the intellectual, right? Does it bother him too?" Amanda understood how sibling roles could manifest, even without anyone trying to do it to be negative. That's how she'd ended up as the sensible one nobody worried about.

A role she'd disliked until the focus turned on her after her recent accident and suddenly every-one fussed over her. She disliked that more.

"We're guys. We've never sat down and talked about our feelings much. But you might have a point. Never thought of it that way."

"Families are funny. Even when you're close, there are always dynamics that impact us in ways we aren't always clear about. I just hope your dad sees how smart you are."

Jake shrugged. "Like I said, he's proud I'm a firefighter, but I don't think he considers that tak-ing smarts. More like instinct and training."

"That's ridiculous." She grabbed his arm to stop him again. "Now I understand a little more why this degree and promotion are so important to you. And why you don't want to tell them about it until you're done."

And her heart splintered a little more for the little boy who had been made to feel less than simply because he was different.

"Yeah, just easier."

"I get it." She wished she didn't, but she did. "And I'll help you any way I can, okay?"

For a moment, he stared down at her, his impressive height silhouetted against the setting sun and kaleidoscope sky. "Thanks."

The ridiculously long black fringe of lashes framing his dark eyes highlighted the heat in their whisky-dark depths. His gaze dropped to her mouth and her throat immediately grew parched.

Her pulse accelerated. "Jake, about last night…"

His eyes grew hooded. "I'm sorry. I just have to focus on school and…"

"You can't mix business with pleasure?" Every nerve ending tingled as she stared up at him. Wishing he would pull her into his arms and slam that sexy mouth down on hers. Public place and his family down the beach be damned.

He stepped back. "I've got to focus on school right now. School and work."

"I understand. Well, time to get home. Thanks for the afternoon. Have fun with Stella." And there was her answer. Damn it. She'd witnessed the dynamic with his family now. How could she deny that she understood his deep-seated desire to have an objective achievement he thought would please his dad? Although she wasn't sure if his dad would ever be pleased or see things differently, no matter how many hoops Jake jumped through.

Selfishly, she wanted to broadcast to the world she was finally attracted to someone––who was she kidding? She wanted to jump his bones––and he was resisting her. Even though she understood his reasons, part of her wished he found her too damn irresistible and pursued her, no matter the cost.

Regardless, she still believed they could mix business with pleasure. All she needed to do was convince Jake it was possible. Between tutoring and working out together, she'd use her powers of proximity and persuasion. He didn't stand a chance.

# CHAPTER 13

AMANDA NIBBLED ON HER FINGERNAIL and studied Jake's strong profile. A hint of five o' clock shadow darkened his square jaw, despite the early hour. He'd texted earlier that morning suggesting they go for a hike down at Torrey Pines State Reserve to assess her lower body strength and begin his part of their bargain. He'd insisted on driving so she didn't have to be concerned with her shoulder. Who was she to argue, even though she'd driven herself to the beach the prior day? Gazing at him instead of focusing on the road certainly wasn't a hardship.

Although she could run for miles and had excellent endurance, her stability obviously needed work. Just ask Cowgirl. More than improving her physical strength, she'd been unable to resist spending more time with Jake. He was easy to hang out with and a friendship was growing between them.

The more time they spent together fulfilling their bargain, the more apparent it would become how they could have the best of both worlds. She wanted to have fun and wasn't looking for long-term, especially with someone with a dangerous career. He had a full plate with work and school, but even the busiest guys would jump at the chance for no-strings sex, right?

Jake Cruz was fully capable of studying, doing well in school, succeeding at his job, and spending time with her. She was sure of it and she'd make it her mission to show him. It would take several sessions of tutoring and personal training to fulfill their bargain. And she did need to get stronger.

Her gaze dropped to where his long tanned fingers lightly gripped the truck's steering wheel. His eyes were hidden behind aviator sunglasses. He was so handsome and those sinewy forearms begged to be touched. To be safe, she swung her gaze out the window and drank in the rugged California coastline as they cruised down the large hill toward the Torrey Pines State Reserve. She'd never tire of this gorgeous coastline and once again she questioned why she hadn't spent more time at the beach when it was so close by. Unlike the bright sun and brilliant blue sky just a few miles inland at the ranch, clouds streaked along the horizon like a pastel watercolor. The marine layer drifted up from the chilly Pacific and temperatures along the coast tended to be cooler. Although the beach was less than ten miles from Pacific Vista Ranch, Amanda felt like she was spreading her wings in a whole new world.

"There's a spot. Right up there. Hurry." Amanda pointed toward a silver Prius with its turn signal flashing. Parking was notoriously tough on this stretch of Highway 101 and if you saw an opening, you swooped in fast.

"Score." Jake expertly maneuvered the truck into the spot.

"Nice parking job." Did he drive the fire engine too? Suddenly Amanda wanted to see Jake in his navy work uniform. Well, maybe just the pants portion. Her cheeks flushed. She was no better than all those screaming women in the *Magic Mike* movies when Jake's doppelganger stripped out of his fireman costume.

"Thanks." He flashed a grin.

The salty breeze caressed her cheeks while they walked along the beach road. They paused at the base of the massive hill leading up to the bluffs and hiking trails. "When's the last time you hiked Torrey Pines?"

Amanda bit her lip. "Don't laugh, but I haven't been here since my last year at UCSD."

Her alma mater, University of California, San Diego, was located a few miles beyond Torrey Pines on the scenic road into downtown La Jolla. As an undergrad, she'd often stopped to hike on her way home from classes. It was easy, convenient, and most importantly, an efficient use of her time. But once she'd left for vet school and then returned to the ranch, she'd settled into her daily routine and didn't often venture out of Rancho Santa Fe.

He stopped and his mouth dropped open. "What? It's like ten miles away."

She shrugged her good shoulder. "I know. I

know. I told you I'd been stuck in a rut. I'm boring, what can I say?"

"You could never be boring. But years?" His
dark brows disappeared underneath his baseball
cap.

Time to change the subject. "So what's on the
agenda? Just a hike?"

His lips hitched up. "Oh, it'll be more than just
a hike. There are tons of spots on Razor Point
trail where we can stop for calisthenics. We obviously won't do burpees or push-ups, but we can
do squats, lunges, and core work. Think intervals."

She gazed over at him. He wore a long sleeved
performance t-shirt tucked into thin black sweats
and looked incredible. The breeze blew the thin
fabric against him, revealing the curve of his
sculpted pecs, the ridges of his abs, and the consid-
erable bulge in his pants. A shiver sparked down
her spine considering just how all that rock-hard
muscle would feel against her. She forced herself
to peer around him to admire the curling white-
capped waves crashing on the beach.

"Amanda? You with me?" His Chargers hat and
mirrored sunglasses concealed his expression.

"Of course. It's just so gorgeous down here.
Let's do this." She fell into step alongside him.

The initial incline––oh darn, she'd forgotten
how steep the ascent to the cliffs actually was.
Thank goodness she'd run for years and wasn't
already out of breath unlike some of the people
toiling alongside them. Sweat prickled on the

back of her neck when the temperature jumped about ten degrees the moment the hill cut off the ocean breeze. Her quads protested, but she directed her focus on keeping her left arm and shoulder relatively quiet so she didn't exacerbate her injuries. Once they'd crested the first hill and curved around closer toward the sharp bluffs, she paused and her breath caught in her throat.

The raw beauty slammed into her. "I'd forgotten how incredible it is here."

Rugged green hills dotted with Torrey pines, cactus, and gold-and-paprika colored wildflowers framed the majestic turquoise Pacific. Gulls squawked overhead and monarch butterflies flitted along the shrubs. The breeze caressed her again, and rays from the mild February sun kissed her skin.

"Doing okay?" Jake gazed down at her.

"Just admiring the view." She looked up at him. *And not just Mother Nature, you sexy beast.*

"It's incredible." He stared down at her for a moment, the pulse in his strong throat visible against his smooth bronzed skin.

The heat of his gaze seared her and despite the resurgence of the wind, warmth flooded her body. The breeze picked up and her nipples leapt to attention. She prayed the padding in her sports bra was enough to disguise them. When he hissed out a sharp exhale, it was apparent the padding was too thin.

Maybe she didn't mind if he could see her response to him because his reaction was gratifying. He blew out another breath and pivoted toward the trails.

"Let's start down Razor Point Trail." Jake's voice was huskier than usual.

She wasn't the only one getting turned on this morning. "Is that the one that leads to the beach or the one on the other side?"

"The one heading north, with the viewpoint at the edge of the bluffs."

The trail was blessedly quiet. The sandy gravelly path crunched beneath their feet, the large winter surf crashed in the distance, and the flutter of birds punctuated the cool, crisp air. Heaven. What a clear reminder that peace and natural beauty existed outside of Pacific Vista Ranch. Amanda inhaled and worked not to scold herself for missing out all these years.

They rounded a sharp bend in the winding path. "Let's go over here for interval number one." Jake headed down a side-path that opened to a tiny clearing. "Lunge squat combos."

"Can you show me?" She leaned against the short expanse of split-rail fence. Why would she miss out on the opportunity to see him perform the moves?

"Sure." He stood with his hands on his hips and lunged his right foot forward, dipping down so his left knee almost touched the earth. The thin material of his sweatpants stretched across his perfect ass and she could swear she saw carved hip dimples flex as he moved.

He pressed up and stepped the right foot out to

the side and squatted back, now giving her yet another spectacular angle to admire his perfect ass. Amanda's heart was thundering against her ribs and her mouth was dry. Good lord.

He angled his head to look at her. "Do it with me."

She inhaled sharply. "Do it with you?"

He cocked his head. "Yes, lunge squat combos. You can use the fence for balance if you need it. Unless you want me to watch your form first?"

She shook her head and laughed nervously. *Please don't let him be able to read my smutty little mind.* "Let's do them together."

They completed a set of fifteen in almost perfect unison and Amanda was careful to keep her gaze glued on the pounding waves and not ogle his powerful thighs and butt. She focused on her breath and the exercise. The flush in her cheeks could be attributed to effort, right?

"A few more sets like that and nobody will knock you over again." He smiled down at her and they continued back onto the trail.

They descended the path, curving past Red Butte lookout point and continuing downhill toward Razor Point. To the south, Scripps Pier and the small peninsula of La Jolla stood out in sharp relief to the azure sky. Amanda was beginning to wonder if her plan to spend time together was backfiring more on her. She seemed to be the one getting flustered and he seemed all cool, calm, and collected. *Focus on the environment and the present moment, girl.* Jake's presence next to her felt as natural and solid as the ancient carved hills they traversed.

A flicker in the waves caught her eye. "Isn't it whale season? Are those whales?" Talking about wildlife was safe, like discussing politics in Switzerland.

Jake kept his gaze fastened on the horizon. It had to be safer to look for whales than to fight staring at Amanda. Of course she looked sexy as hell in a pair of gray sweats and a pale pink thermal t-shirt. A paper-thin pink thermal t-shirt. When the breeze had picked up earlier, he'd almost lost control and pulled her into his arms and dragged her off somewhere private. Like behind a bush.

How was he going to be able to maintain a personal trainer attitude with her? Maybe some of those blinders they put on horses would help?

Something broke through the water's surface and he jerked to a stop. Amanda bumped into the back of him and he stiffened. Damn it. Even just an innocent brush against his body practically undid him. They were fully clothed, for god's sake.

Focus on the whales. Nature. The ocean. All that.

He stepped forward, carefully putting some space between them. A safety net. "There are a few whales out there. Can you see them?" He pointed north toward Del Mar.

Another spout blew and the slightest hint of a

tail appeared soon after. "Oh my gosh, yes. Can we go closer?"

"Let's do it. Just know we'll do some core work once they've finished swimming by. Deal?" They hurried down to Razor Point, on the very edge of the cliffs, where they'd have the best view of the whales breaching and surfacing.

She laughed. "You're a drill sergeant. Hurry up. I don't want to miss them."

He followed her, keeping his gaze out on the water as much as he could. But the sway of her narrow hips was beyond distracting. "Like you weren't as a tutor."

She glanced back. "Hey, I wasn't a drill sergeant. I just wanted you to get good grades. And you did." Had she been too tough on him?

"Kidding. You were the best teacher I ever had." And the most beautiful. And the most patient.

When they reached the split rail fence at the edge of the cliff, they drank in the frolicking of the whales, swimming close to the shoreline below. Pods swam south from Alaska to Mexico to have babies.

"Oh, good. You scared me for a minute." She smiled at him and a strand of golden hair escaped her braid and blew across her lips.

Before he could think, he reached up and brushed the silky strands away and his knuckles grazed her full, unpainted mouth. He froze.

She grasped his wrist, holding him in place. Without breaking eye contact, she lowered her head and brushed her lips against the palm of his hand, searing him with her velvet touch. She released his hand and shifted her gaze out to the horizon, her profile serene.

Like she hadn't just branded him with her kiss.

His fingers curled in and he squeezed. Hard. His feet refused to budge and he sucked in an inhale and blew out an exhale. How was he supposed to resist her? How did he resist the dream come to life with warm flesh, soft sweet breath, and an eager response beyond his wildest imagination? *Think fast.*

"Should we keep going or do you want to watch the whales a little longer?" She asked, her voice steady. Like she hadn't just blown his mind.

"Core work. On the bench." He managed the words between clenched teeth.

She stared at the carved wooden bench and flicked her gaze back up at him. Her green eyes were hidden behind her sunglasses. "Seriously?" Those pink lips formed a perfect O and his jaw clicked shut.

"Yeah, seriously. Lie down on your back, with your hips on the edge of the bench." Because seeing her on her back with her legs extended up in the air was definitely going to keep his imagination contained. Damn.

She complied and he had her run through a series of leg lifts and reverse crunches, careful to keep his eyes focused on her tennis shoes and not her long, slender thighs. He breathed through his nose, struggling to maintain his composure.

"Aren't you doing a set too?" Her voice was

breathy now, even more alluring.

"Already worked out. Let's move on." He started down the path because if she saw his body's reaction to her, he'd have no secrets. And the sway of her gentle curves walking in front of him might send him over the edge.

Jake couldn't stop opening and closing his fingers on the hand where she'd kissed him. She sauntered along the narrow twists and turns, performing the calisthenics intervals with him as if nothing had happened. Just like they were trainer and client on a fitness hike. What the hell?

He kept his eyes fixed on the path and stuffed that kiss into the vault to retrieve later and ponder, analyze, and replay. Probably in one of many ice-cold showers. That feather light touch of her mouth would haunt him for the foreseeable future.

He appreciated the quiet camaraderie with her walking by his side. Some of the women he'd dated felt the need to talk and talk and talk because he wasn't much of a conversationalist. Not that he didn't enjoy discussing subjects that interested him or explore new ones; he just didn't feel the need to chat about inane topics in order to feel comfortable. He'd existed the first twenty-seven years of his life with lots of silence and liked it that way.

Maybe he and Amanda had more in common than he thought.

But what they did or didn't have in common was beside the point. When he was near her, her presence consumed all of his senses. Dangerous.

The trail widened, allowing them to walk side by side. "Thanks for getting me back out to Torrey Pines. I forgot how much I love it here. And the whales were such a bonus." Amanda smiled up at him.

"Right? We can definitely come here again." Jake said. But if she could wear baggy sweats, it would make it less painful for him.

"But no rock climbing here?"

He shook his head. "Well, you aren't even going to be rock climbing in the gym until your doctor signs off after your physical therapy. But no. We'll have to go out east."

Lightness flowed through him on the walk down the hill toward the beach. The wind had picked up and blown away the few clouds along the pristine perfection of the shoreline. Even though he'd been aroused through half the hike, somehow being with Amanda filled him with a calmness he wasn't used to experiencing. Something about her was comforting. Which made no sense when almost everything she did turned him on.

She pouted, looking young, sulky, and absolutely adorable. "Stupid shoulder."

He laughed. "Being injured is the worst. It's just for a little while."

"Easy for you to say when you're all big and strong and tough." She flicked one slender hand in the air.

"You're tough too, Amanda. Don't be so hard on yourself." Listen to him echoing the advice she gave to him.

She shrugged. "It's just frustrating. But I don't want to whine about it. I need to get back to the ranch for work anyway. You've still got some time off, right?"

When they reached the car, he opened her door. "Time off from the fire station, but I'll be making flash cards like my boss told me."

She snorted. "Boss. Just call me Boss Lady from now on."

"Will do, Boss Lady." He grinned and gunned the truck for Pacific Vista Ranch.

Being with Amanda was easy. Could he actually study, do well in school, and see her too? When he was with her this morning, it seemed like anything was possible. But if the relationship turned romantic, concentrating on anything but her would test his limits. Being Amanda McNeill's man seemed more like the pinnacle in life than becoming fire captain.

"Okay, on a serious note, you talk to your advisor tomorrow, right?" She shifted in the passenger seat, crossing one long leg.

He gulped and nodded. *Think about school, not those sexy walking sticks.* No matter how much fun they'd had and no matter how comfortable he felt with her, he needed to remain focused.

"Do you want me to come over tomorrow night and help you review to retake the test? That way I can take Stella home with me so you don't have to leave too early Tuesday morning?"

He glanced over at her again, and his chest tightened. Her consideration and sweetness blew him away. Somehow she seemed even more gorgeous than he remembered. He wasn't a little boy enamored with his tutor anymore, now he was a man getting to know Amanda McNeill, the woman. Not just simply her big brain and external beauty.

"Are you sure? Aren't you guys in busy season?"

Her lips turned down at the corners. "Yeah. We are. But we've brought on a local vet to help out for the next few months. So I'll have more free time than I usually would."

"Lucky for me." *More like tempting and dangerous.*

Her lips twitched. "I'd hold off on calling yourself lucky until after we've prepped for your test. Especially once I see how sore my legs are tomorrow from your workout."

"I'm lucky to have you any way I can." He blew out a long breath and smiled.

Her eyebrows arched. "We'll see."

When he pulled up to Pacific Vista Ranch, Scott the guard waved him in, like he was a part of the family.

He parked in front of her home, and hopped out to open her passenger side door. She smiled, stepped out of the truck, and stroked her hand along his arm. Adrenaline coursed through his veins and every muscle in his body stiffened.

"Thanks again for taking me. We'll have to go to Torrey Pines again." Her pink lips curved up.

"Definitely." Right now, he couldn't refuse if she requested a ride to Mars. "If you're sure about tomorrow, how does six o'clock sound?"

She cocked her head and gazed into his eyes.

"Perfect. And Jake?"

"Yeah?"

"Tell your brother not to drop by." With a wicked grin, she turned on her heel and strode to the front door.

Jake's jaw dropped open. Well then.

Tomorrow night was going to be interesting.

# CHAPTER 14

AMANDA SMOOTHED HER HAIR AWAY from her face and inhaled a deep cleansing breath. She felt confident in her plan. Confident seducing Jake was the right thing to do. Confident they'd be able to have a personal relationship while being successful in every other area of their lives as well. Jake might not trust himself to do well, but she knew he had it in him. And somehow the world seemed lighter with Jake in her life.

She didn't even mind Leo doing her job.

Well, didn't mind Leo doing her job as much as she'd anticipated. She'd carefully outlined exact procedures for how she ran the practice and it took every ounce of her self-control not to stand over his shoulder and supervise his work.

No doubt she'd have to go back and correct a million things.

She exhaled and shook her head. No need to fret about her career tonight. It was temporary. The ranch wasn't going anywhere.

Now she was at Jake's, wearing her sexiest lingerie underneath her jeans and casual cardigan sweater. The deep, forest green scraps of silk bolstered her confidence and reinforced her decision to make the first move this evening. She couldn't shake the memory of Jake's expression after she'd kissed his palm. He'd been flummoxed. If tonight went as she planned, they'd both be smiling.

All night.

Stella would be happy to have both of them under the same roof. Because if all went well this evening, Amanda wasn't going home until tomorrow morning.

She knocked on the door and it flew open immediately.

Jake stood silhouetted in the doorway. "Hi Amanda." His voice sounded huskier than usual.

His thick black hair was shower damp, a white t-shirt stretched across his sculpted solid chest and hinted at the ridges of abdominals where it tucked into faded jeans. Possibly the most beautiful decoration on all 6'5 inches of pure rock-hard muscle. His feet were bare and somehow his toes were sexy too. She swallowed.

"Hi." Was her voice really that breathy? So much for being the seductress when simply looking at him and two words out of his mouth rendered her tongue-tied.

He reached one powerful arm out and clasped her hand. "Come on in. I'm ready for flashcards." With one gentle tug, she was inside his apartment.

Her tummy took a long languorous roll and a warm tingle started at her scalp and traveled down her spine. Her heartbeat hitched and suddenly she didn't feel so much like the one in charge, as she'd anticipated when she'd gotten ready for this evening. The door clicked shut behind her and Amanda's heart knocked faster against her ribcage.

Stella leapt up and ran over with an excited yip and greeted her. Amanda sighed in relief. Animals she was comfortable around. She needed to pull herself together before she chickened out of her plan.

"Someone seems to be feeling better." Amanda crouched down next to the dog and scratched her ears. Stella's tail thundered against the hardwood floor and her tongue lolled out of the side of her mouth.

She ran her hands over the dog's chest and flanks and smiled up at Jake. "She's healing so fast. She's a lucky girl."

"I'm feeling lucky you're here too." Jake looked down at her, his expression unreadable.

Amanda laughed. Soon they'd both be lucky, if the evening went as she anticipated. Study first. "Well, reviewing flash cards definitely involves luck. You ready?"

He hesitated for a moment and reached out a hand and helped her to her feet. "Yeah, I figured we could sit on the couch and you could quiz me. Can I get you a beer? Or some wine?"

The hair on the back of her neck stood at attention from the heat radiating where their fingers connected. "I'll wait until school time is over, deal?"

"That's smart. Let's do this." He released her hand and they settled down on opposite ends of his oversized charcoal colored leather couch.

She picked up the stack of index cards from the coffee table and quickly skimmed them. "You did a great job breaking this down. But first, what did your advisor and teacher say? I'm assuming you've got another chance?"

He nodded. "Yeah, I do. I told them I'd gotten some assistance with studying and they said it wasn't really uncommon for people like me to have a rough start in the program."

She stiffened. "What do you mean, people like you?"

His lips twitched up. "Oh, they just mean with firefighters and people who've been out of high school for several years. They know it can be a tough re-entry."

Her shoulders softened. Although she wanted him to have allowances for his processing challenges, her protective instincts stirred. "That makes sense. Let's get you prepped to retake the test. And then you can use the flashcards on the rest of your exams if they make a difference for you."

They reviewed the flashcards for an hour or so and Jake demonstrated mastery over the material. She'd been correct: they could study together and stay focused on the work, as opposed to their attraction. Granted, sitting on opposite ends of the couch helped because he wasn't within arms' reach. Safer that way.

Once she was satisfied they'd covered everything thoroughly, her awareness shifted from schoolwork to the man. "How are you feeling now? Ready to take the test without needing luck?"

His eyes darkened and he nodded his head. For a moment they stared at each other. "Like I said, I can always use a little luck. Wine?" He rose from the couch.

Amanda looked away for a moment and gathered her courage. Squaring her shoulders, she stood, and gazed up into his hot dark eyes. Exhaled an unsteady breath. Carpe Diem and all that, right? She was taking charge of her life and that included making the first move with Jake tonight.

"How about we both get lucky?" She held her breath.

Jake stared at her for a moment, his eyes hooded, his mouth pressed into a tight line.

For an endless moment, their gazes remained locked and nerves danced along her skin. She licked her lips.

He slid one large hand around the nape of her neck, pulled her in close, then swooped in and claimed her mouth. His tongue swept around hers and she wrapped her arms around his narrow waist and dragged him even closer. Her breasts were crushed against his rock-hard abs and his obvious arousal dug into her. Her eyelids floated shut and she murmured his name.

With a growl, he swept her up into his powerful arms, careful of her shoulder, and fused his mouth to hers. Without breaking the kiss, he carried her to his bedroom, and gently sat her on the edge of his enormous bed.

He released her mouth, knelt between her legs, and smoothed her hair away from her flushed face. Every stroke of his fingers singed her skin. Every inch of her body flamed and liquid heat pooled in her center.

"Is your shoulder okay, beautiful?" He trailed his lips down her throat, pausing to press openmouthed heated kisses along her collarbone.

His sweetness and pure consideration for her well-being made her even hotter.

Her head lolled off to the side as she allowed him full access to her neck. Sparks were shooting directly from the sensitive spot just beneath her ear straight to her center. He continued kissing down across the top of her chest, and then suddenly pulled away. She moaned in protest.

"Shhh, I've got to see you." He unbuttoned her sweater and for a moment, he froze in place, his obsidian eyes gleaming as he looked at her bare torso. He tossed her top over his shoulder.

Keeping her pinned with his dark gaze, he slid off one silk strap and leaned down to breathe in her skin. "You smell like the beach, like sunshine and surf wax and sugar." He brushed his slightly open mouth across her skin, leaning down to kiss along the top of her breasts over the cups of her bra.

Somehow the other strap was down around her arm and he was nibbling on her like she was the sweetest treat he'd ever sampled. He lowered his mouth and captured one breast, scraping her nipple through the silk, with just enough pressure to force another moan from her.

Her mind was buzzing and everywhere he touched burned.

What was he doing to her? "Please…" She grasped his thick, unruly hair in her hands.

"Please what?" His raspy voice murmured against her sensitive skin.

"Please kiss me." Was he trying to kill her?

"Kiss you where?" He leaned back and gazed at her from his position between her spread thighs, his mouth just a breath away from her breasts.

"My breasts. Kiss my breasts." *Please.*

He growled again. Suddenly her bra was sailing over his shoulder and he lowered his mouth to her breast, flicking his tongue over and over across her nipple. His large rough palms glided up and spanned her ribcage, holding her in place while he drove her mad. Teasing, licking, biting until she begged for more.

One strong hand slid around to her back and the other brushed along her stomach and his fingers grazed along the waistband of her jeans. He cupped her through her jeans and she arched back, eager for the barriers between them to dissolve.

"Jake, I——"

He lowered his head and his mouth followed the trail from her breasts down to the waistband of her pants. His large hand splayed against her lower back supported her or she would have collapsed flat onto his bed. He seized the fabric between his teeth, held her in place, and slid the zipper down. Cool air caressed her skin when he shifted to stroke her through her silk panties.

He groaned. "You're so wet for me, Amanda. So hot."

She strained against his hand, her breath coming in harsh pants now. "Please. More."

He shifted back, peeled her jeans off, and tossed them over his shoulder to join the rest of her clothes. He slid his square palms down the inside of her thighs and pressed them apart, his grip firm. She struggled to open her eyes halfway—her eyelids were so heavy—and looked at him.

He was staring at her, his dark eyes hooded, his full lips parted. He was the most beautiful man she'd ever seen.

"Jake." If he didn't touch her or kiss her or take her, she might burst.

Without releasing her gaze, he came closer, inch by inch, and brushed his hot mouth from the inside of her knee up to where she was burning for him. Watching his dark head move along her pale skin mesmerized her.

"I'm going to taste you now. Kiss you and lick you until you scream my name when you come." His voice was a low purr.

Her head dropped back. "Yes. Now. Do it now."

He tasted her in one long powerful stroke of his tongue and she bowed up off the bed, every nerve ending electrified. Everything else fell away, except for the pleasure surging through her body, hot and thrilling. She thrust her fingers into his thick, silky hair, held his head in place, and writhed beneath him. When he shifted his attentions to her most sensitive part and slid two long fingers inside her, she exploded, his name on her lips.

He continued to press light kisses around her center until the tremors subsided and she went limp. He climbed up onto the bed next to her, propped his dark head on one elbow, and brushed his fingertips lightly across her body. A devilish grin curved his lips upward as goosebumps erupted wherever he touched.

"Are you laughing at me?" She smiled up at him. He could keep petting her like this forever. But she wanted more.

More of him.

All of him.

"I wouldn't dare." His grin deepened, his eyes crinkling at the corners.

She rolled onto to her right side and pressed up to seated. When he started to rise, she pushed him back onto his back. "My turn."

His eyes widened and the flush darkening his skin intensified. "You're still hurt, Amanda. I just wanted to make you feel good."

"Take off your shirt, please. Actually, take everything off. That will make me feel good." Powerful. Supremely female.

After two seconds, he popped up. He whipped off his t-shirt, shucked his jeans and boxers, and was on his back in a heartbeat.

A laugh escaped her. "Wow, you're fast."

"One of the benefits of my line of work: you

learn to change clothes fast." Male satisfaction shone in his smile and he reclined back, his arms crossed behind his head.

She looked at him. Really looked at him and every bit of humor evaporated, along with any moisture in her mouth. *Sweet lord above.* Nothing could have prepared her for the visual of his perfectly sculpted physique, not even watching *Magic Mike* on repeat.

No, he was a real life Adonis. Bronzed skin stretched over solid muscles, sinewy and athletic, from his broad shoulders, solid chest, his six or eight or who knows how many-pack, to his powerful thighs. His erection was massive and was definitely in proportion to the rest of him. She swallowed over her parched throat again, a little worried about how *that* could possibly fit inside of her.

But she'd worry about that in a bit. She had to touch. She had to taste.

It was only fair.

She crawled up and kissed him, eagerly swirling her tongue against his. When he started to move his arms, she stopped him. "No, keep your arms where they are."

His eyes narrowed and his jaw clenched. "You don't want me to touch you?"

"Not until I tell you to. Let me explore you at my own pace." She smiled down at him. "You know, because of my injury."

He stiffened. Everywhere. But he didn't move.

She balanced on her knees next to him and bent

down to skim her lips across his chest and scrape his tight dark nipples. He sucked in a deep breath, but remained still while she explored him. She braced herself with one hand on solid, rock-hard muscle, traveled down the planes of his carved stomach, and paused at the indentation of his navel. She inhaled the scent of his smooth skin, a combination of soap and something male. Something delicious.

A thin trail of dark hair lead down to his cock and she curled her fingers around his girth and stroked him from base to tip. His hips jerked up, his breath coming in erratic pants now.

She turned and looked up. He watched her with hooded eyes, his white teeth digging into his full lower lip. Keeping her gaze locked with his, her lips repeated the path her hand had traveled, licking him from base to tip. He growled.

"Amanda." His voice was guttural. Deep.

Smiling, she took him into her mouth, relaxing her throat so she could take as much of him in as possible. She pleasured him with her mouth and her hands and savored every flinch and muttered curse he uttered. Power existed in taking charge. Power existed in giving him what he'd so willingly given her.

A hand stroked through her hair. "Come up here. Please."

She slid up his body, now glistening with sweat, and he engulfed her in the power of his arms. He captured her mouth with his, a new urgency in his kiss. His hands stroked down her back and caught her hips.

She shifted in his arms, working to ease down on him. "I want you inside me."

He slid his hands up her waist to clasp her face in his hands. "Are you sure? I don't want to hurt you." His erection was digging into her thigh and the control he managed to show was herculean. His eyes flickered with uncertainty.

"I'm tougher than I look." Her chest tightened at his protectiveness. She buried her face into his neck and grazed him with her teeth. "I want you."

Before she could move another muscle, he'd lifted her up like she weighed nothing and set her to the side. "Don't move."

He scrambled to his nightstand and she admired the carved grooves on the side of his round glutes as he grabbed a condom. He tore the packet and tossed it over his shoulder, probably to join all their clothes he'd thrown across the room tonight. She bit her lip, eager for him to return to her.

He picked her up, reclined onto his back, and placed her so she was straddling him. She moaned and rubbed herself against him, unable to resist the heat where they touched.

"Help me put it on." He uttered through gritted teeth.

Together they unrolled the condom and covered every inch of him. With one smooth move, he lifted her so she was poised with him pressing against her entrance. Her legs trembled and tingles shot along her spine.

With their gazes locked together, he lowered

her on top of him slowly. She moaned each time he paused to allow her to adjust to him stretching her wide. Had she ever felt so deliciously full? So incredibly complete? Her head dropped back, her back arched, and she moaned her pleasure.

Once she was seated fully, he reached for her hand, winding their fingers together. He gripped her hip with the other hand and they began to move. She rode him, increasing the pace, and sounds of their shared moans permeated the room. Their skin grew slippery and slick and each stroke filled her with pleasure. When he reached forward and pressed his thumb where they were connected, she exploded, waves of pleasure riding over her. He clasped her hips, thrust up power-fully, and cried her name as he flew over the edge and joined her.

Boneless and satiated beyond her wildest imagi-nation, Amanda collapsed onto his firm chest. His hands stroked through her tangled hair, down her spine, across her hips, and hugged her close. The wild beating of her heart echoed his and her lips curved up along his smooth skin. The cradle of his arms felt like she'd come home.

# CHAPTER 15

JAKE RESTED HIS HEAD IN his hand and watched Amanda begin to awaken. Streaks of sunlight peeked over the dark curtains, highlighting her staggering beauty. Her mouth was swollen and pink from their passionate kisses, her hair a wild mass of tousled gold against his navy sheets, her creamy skin still flushed from the steamy shower they'd shared in the middle of the night.

It was only six a.m. and they hadn't slept much. A satisfied smile spread across his face. Last night had been the best night of his life. Not just the best sex of his life——every fantasy he'd had about Amanda McNeill from the time he was a horny teenager couldn't begin to compare to the passionate, generous, incredible lover she was in reality. And he'd felt comfortable with her. Natural. No awkward silences, no silences at all. Who would have guessed the serene doctor would be so vocal?

So loud and demanding and wild?

He had the bite marks to prove it.

And now every part of him was fully awake and ready to go.

Unfortunately he had to be at the station soon.

He'd never called in sick before, but playing hooky with the lovely woman resting in his bed tempted him. Maybe he could make up an excuse and head in a few hours late.

He frowned. Damn it, he'd vowed to keep their relationship platonic so he could focus on work and school. After one night with Amanda, he already wanted to chuck his responsibilities to lounge around with her. Not a good sign.

"I didn't expect to wake up to an unhappy man this morning." The last remnants of sleep lent huskiness to her soft voice. She gazed up at him through her long lashes, her green eyes hooded.

He tucked a silky strand of hair behind her ear and smiled at her. "Not unhappy. Just the opposite. But duty calls."

"What time is it?" She sighed and sat up, and the sheet covering her slipped so one rosy nipple peeked up at him. Tempted him to stroke her silky skin. Waking up with her was heaven and hell. If only it was one of his days off, he'd strip the sheet off and time would fall away again. But he forced himself to get out of bed.

"Six."

She groaned, straightened, and scooted to the edge of the bed. "Oh shoot, I've got to get home. Sam's expecting me down at the barn at seven sharp."

"I thought the other vet was handling your job?" Wasn't she supposed to be taking it easy?

She looked around the room, her slender back to him. "Not all of it. I'm handling a lot of the lab work today. My delicate shoulder's fine there."

"Your clothes are on the dresser. I moved them off the floor last night." And seeing the skimpy silky lingerie again reminded him just how incredible she'd looked wearing it.

Amanda laughed. "Well, you were the one tossing them all over the room."

"You complaining?" He crossed his arms over his chest and raised his eyebrows.

"How soon do you have to be at the station again?" She raked her gaze along his body, and no way could she miss the tenting of his thin sweatpants.

Damn she was sexy. But he couldn't be late to work, not if he was on track to be captain one day.

"I really want to make you breakfast, but I've got to be at work."

Her lips curved up. "You're sweet. I've got to run too, my sister runs a tight ship. Rain check?"

His shoulders relaxed. Maybe he should lighten up. "Definitely."

She gathered her clothes and headed into the bathroom. He scrubbed his hands through his hair and grabbed his work clothes. He'd spent the most amazing night with Amanda and he wasn't going to screw it up by over-thinking it.

He wasn't the only one with a schedule——she was a busy veterinarian. This morning she seemed comfortable and casual about last night. If she could play it cool and they each focused on their careers and spent their free time together, maybe he could take it day by day. His dream woman was now his and he didn't want to let her go.

Jake hadn't thought anything could have ruined his perfect mood, but trying to choke down the egg white frittata his co-worker had made for breakfast duty this morning at the station was killing his buzz. Bill Moyer, resident killjoy, was on the latest fad diet, which touted getting more ripped than ever before, and as a result was making the rest of them suffer through his crap recipes. Could he have thrown in at least one yolk? Maybe a little bit of salt? Because this meal tasted blander than unseasoned tofu. Oh yeah, because the frittata was full of plain tofu and some tasteless unidentifiable pale green vegetables.

He'd kill for some salsa right about now, to help choke down the rest of the dish, or hell, even some salt and pepper would help. He gulped down some water and glanced around. The rest of the crew were picking at their plates like it was liver and onions night at the grandparents'.

"Dude, not sure what this was today, but next time you're on breakfast, can you give us some cheese or whole eggs or something? If we get called out today, I might faint from starvation," Matthews said. He was a former college linebacker, sitting at the far end of the family-style oak table. And he'd summed up what all of them were thinking.

Moyer, one of the senior fire engineers at Rancho Santa Fe Station #1, whipped his head toward

Matthews, his bushy eyebrows knit together. "We're supposed to be in prime shape and if you want to shovel in pancakes and donuts, you won't last long around here. This frittata is full of protein, so if you faint it's because you're a pussy."

Jake sighed. Moyer was a prick. Challenge him and he'd attack. Every time.

"Lay off, Moyer. Just because you're trying to fit into a banana hammock this summer doesn't mean the rest of us have to eat like the Real Housewives of Rancho Santa Fe." Parks, one of the newer guys still in his probationary period, piped in from next to Matthews.

Snickers erupted around the table. Nobody liked Moyer and his self-righteous habits, even if he was excellent in the field. He managed to keep some of his most annoying behavior hidden from the captain and chief, but the rest of the crew saw it on the regular. Jake swallowed his own chuckle, not wanting to get in the middle or become the target. He'd had enough of being a target as a kid, so he steered clear of the guy as much as possible.

"Shut it, Parks. Would hate to see you get let go, since you're still on probation."

"Like you've got any control over that." Parks narrowed his eyes.

"I don't know, the captain talks to me. Asks me about everything going on when he's not around. I'd watch my mouth if I were you." A sneer marred Moyer's face, transforming him from ordinary to ugly.

"Moyer, you've got no more pull than the rest

of us. Parks does a great job." Carson, usually one of the friendliest guys at the station, glared up at him.

"Shut up, Carson. You have no clue what I know. So Parks, if I were you, I'd lick that plate clean."

Jake slammed his hands down on the table. "Enough. This isn't basic training." He looked around the table. "Parks, there's some bread in the top cabinet, how about making us some toast."

Another round of snickers.

"Toast sounds good, at least bread has some flavor." Parks stood and sauntered into the kitchen.

"Seriously, Cruz? You giving orders now? Some of us actually served our country and have some self-discipline." Moyer stood up, his past military training evident in his ramrod straight posture.

Jake ground his back teeth together. Now the stick-up-his-ass jerk was going to go all prima donna on him? Seriously? He took a few deep breaths. He was accustomed to Moyer talking shit. And if he wanted to be fire captain, he couldn't let bullies trigger his temper.

"Moyer, you're a stupid prick. Lay off Cruz." Carson warned.

"It's okay guys. Moyer, why don't you use that self-discipline and stop being so sensitive about what people want to eat for breakfast. We've got more important things to focus on around here." Jake looked around the table and his heart warmed to see the rest of the team nodding in agreement with him. "If you guys are still hungry, I'll scramble up some eggs to go with that toast."

He rose and walked into the kitchen, adrenaline pumping through his veins, half ready for Moyer to tackle him from behind. What he'd learned from all the years of being mocked as a kid was walking away was the only way to defuse the situation. So, if Moyer didn't get the attention, the fun went out of being an asshole. But for all he knew, the guy enjoyed being an asshole for the sake of it.

Everyone filed in after him, except for Moyer. Thank god. He didn't need the confrontation. That guy thrived on stirring up trouble and if Jake wanted to be captain of this station, he needed to play it cool and stay out of the guy's path. Be the bigger man.

Carson slapped him on the back. "Way to shut that jerk down. And please make some eggs for us. Parks found some onions and tomatoes."

"Sure." Although knowing Moyer, he'd pay for making a second breakfast. But he was frickin' starving too. Egg white tofu surprise wasn't going to cut it today.

Jake stared out the window at the clear cobalt sky from his seat in the upstairs lounge. Because the station had been unusually quiet following the ridiculous breakfast scene, his mind kept darting between wondering what Amanda was doing and what she was wearing—yeah, he was pathetic. He checked his phone, on the off chance Amanda had texted him. Damn. Not a single message.

If only he could study at the station, he'd have somewhere else to focus his attention. As Amanda had directed, he'd copied out all his notes onto index cards with one concept on the front and the answer on the back. It helped. A lot. Taking in the information in small chunks allowed him to memorize it without getting overwhelmed. Last night after she'd quizzed him, his confidence had been bolstered.

And then somehow she'd ended up in his bed—he closed his eyes for a moment and took a few deep breaths. He had twenty-two more hours at the station unless a call came in. If he spent them fantasizing about Amanda, it would feel more like twenty-two hundred.

He would not indulge himself in remembering every incredible second of last night in slow-motion replay. He'd already spent way too much time doing just that. Imagining her soft hot mouth, her silky skin, and long surprisingly strong legs. He shook his head. Work. School. Focus.

The bummer was he couldn't study at the station because of people like Moyer. If that guy had a clue of his ambitions to become captain and to earn his college degree? A worse nightmare than any of the clowns or resurrected animals Stephen King could conceive. No way in hell. Moyer would make fun of him and block him at every turn. No, he would keep his ambitions to himself, do an exemplary job every day, and not reveal his plans until those two initials stood next to his credentials.

"Playing video games on your phone, Cruz? Do they have ones for people as boneheaded as you?" Moyer's sharp voice sounded from over his shoulder.

Jake straightened in his seat. *Do not engage.* "What do you want?"

"Look at me when I talk to you, Cruz."

Jake closed his eyes and counted to five before turning his head to look up at the jerk. But he wasn't a scrawny little kid anymore and he wouldn't take this crap at his adult job. He stood, squared his shoulders, and looked down at Moyer, who didn't quite reach six feet. He didn't respond, simply raised his eyebrows.

When the jerk clued in that he wasn't going to play along, he kept yapping. Didn't he know that whoever spoke first was usually the loser in any negotiation or discussion? Even big "boneheads" knew that.

"Don't ever challenge me that way in front of the team again. Do you understand me?"

Sometimes being 6'5 really came in handy. Jake didn't care if it was petty, he enjoyed that Moyer had to lift his balding ginger head up to address him. He was probably one of the guys claiming to be six feet on online dating apps and always disappointed his unlucky matches.

"Sorry if you thought it was a challenge. We need to be fueled up to go out on calls and some of us need more calories. Don't take it so person-ally." Even though it was personal.

Moyer's nostrils flared and his thin lips flattened. "I'm going to be captain of this station one day and when I am, I'm cleaning house."

Jake shrugged his shoulders. "Don't be so sure. The fire chief looks for someone the station can rally behind."

Moyer smirked. "Yeah, someone like you?"

Jake remained silent. Yeah, someone like him. He had razor sharp reflexes, worked his ass off, and more importantly, the rest of the crew respected and liked him.

"Look, Cruz, big meatheads like you only get the promotions in the movies. We aren't living an action flick and you aren't Vin Diesel." He snickered, apparently cracking himself up.

"You done?" Not reacting was like throwing gasoline onto a fire with guys like Moyer, but Jake refused to stoop to his level and trade insults.

"No comeback? Because you know I'm right. You keep driving the truck and putting out fires. Guys like you are expendable. A dime a dozen. You wait and see." The asshole pivoted and marched out of the room.

Jake sank down onto the chair, dropped his head back, and stared up at the station's ceiling. Maybe it was lack of sleep, but the jerk had managed to hit the mark with his comments.

All his life, he'd earned recognition for being a big strong guy with fast reflexes. While he appreciated being valuable during emergencies, he wanted more. He embodied every characteristic a great captain needed and he would lead a team, inspire other men and women, and be in charge.

He'd prove him wrong. Bill Moyer, asshole number one, would eat every word he'd uttered and then some. Earning his degree was the most important thing he could do to change his life and even make the lives of his co-workers better. Once he graduated, he'd get on the promotion list at the station and that nasty worm would be transferred out of Rancho Santa Fe.

He'd succeed, no matter the sacrifice.

# CHAPTER 16

A MANDA LEANED AGAINST THE STAIN-LESS-STEEL cabinets and enjoyed the chill against her cheek. A wave of tiredness washed through her, but the bone-deep exhaustion had been worth every single second of lost sleep. Last night with Jake surpassed her wildest imagination. Her eyes popped open.

Daydreaming about last night wouldn't help her finish up the daunting amount of shipment-related and administrative tasks she faced this morning. Because she'd had to reassign all her physical duties, Sam had taken the opportunity to dump all the paperwork on her.

Every last little detail, number, statistic, and calculation.

She rubbed the grittiness from her eyes and yawned for what felt like the hundredth time this morning.

"There's my hard-working daughter, sleeping on the job. Did your shoulder keep you up?" Her father's concerned voice jolted her from her sleepy haze.

Amanda straightened up and her eyes widened. Hopefully looked innocent. No smug grins allowed. Although she was a thirty-year-old woman, her dad didn't need to know she'd been up all night riding the firefighter. And oh, what a ride it had been.

Despite the soreness and sleepiness, she couldn't wait to do it again. She forced her attention to the present.

"My shoulder's okay. I've got my first PT this afternoon and hope it helps fast." She massaged her aching joint.

His brows knitted together. "I'm sorry you've got to deal with this. Do you have time to come up to the house for a quick lunch? I need a quick family meeting with you and your sisters."

Amanda's stomach clenched. "Not another movie on the ranch?" The last one had thrown all of their lives into upheaval. Heck, she was just now dealing with the repercussions of all the changes. Better late than never.

Her dad shook his head. "No, I promised you it was a one-time thing. But let's go up to the house so I can share with you all at once. It's good news." He smiled, his hazel eyes crinkling at the corners.

Her tight muscles relaxed. "Sure, let me finish getting these doses in the equitainer and I'll be right up. Do you need me to get Sam?"

"Already told her. You know she never misses a meal, and once I told her Angela made her fried chicken, she ran to the house." He laughed. "Want me to wait?"

She shook her head. "No, I'll be up in a few. Go ahead." She needed to pump another bottle of Visine into her bloodshot eyes and make sure none of the little red marks she'd discovered along her neck and collarbone were visible over her hoodie's neckline. Explaining those away was one more topic she wasn't willing to discuss with anyone.

She shivered remembering the scruff on Jake's square jaw tickling and rasping along every inch of her. Water sluicing along their slick skin as he took her against the shower wall, his powerful physique holding her up while he drove into her. His tenderness when he carried her back to bed and spooned her before falling asleep. Oh yes, Jake Cruz was definitely the right choice for a passionate fling and the first step to kissing her monotonous life goodbye once and for all.

Unable to curb what must be a self-satisfied grin, she finished putting the sample away, double-checked herself in the mirror, and strolled back up for the family meal.

Stella greeted her with a pleased woof from her perch in her dog bed, tucked along the breakfast nook on the far side of the kitchen. She crossed the room to scratch the mutt's ears before going to serve herself from the food laid out on the granite kitchen island.

"There you are. We already started lunch. Let me serve you, I don't want you straining your shoulder." Angela bustled over from the table and grabbed a colorful daffodil plate before Amanda could beat her to it.

"I can feed myself. I'm not an invalid." This fussing over her had to stop.

"Of course you're not an invalid, but don't you want to get better as fast as you can? You know I love to help. Just sit down." Her stepmom beamed at her, her warm brown eyes twinkling.

Recovering from this accident was making one thing crystal clear—being waited on and being treated like she needed assistance didn't agree with her. But perhaps her lack of sleep was making her crankier than usual. She sighed and pulled out a chair—at least they allowed the resident patient to do that. She plopped down between Dylan and Sam, who was eating off her husband Holt's plate. Her little sister's plate was already empty—she had the appetite of a truck driver. As usual, their dad was at the head of the table.

Official family business always took place around the huge farm table and it appeared this afternoon was indeed official business. What now? She looked around the table and everyone was intent on their food. Another McNeill tradition. Her family definitely didn't believe in missing a meal or discussing anything on an empty stomach. Aware nobody would get answers until they'd all finished their meals, she started on her chicken breast.

"Dad, Amanda and I don't have tons of time today because we've got to get back to the barn.

Can you tell us what's going on?" Sam was never one to wait quietly.

Since she and Holt had fallen in love last year, some of her sharp edges had softened. Nobody would call Sam a patient woman, but her fuse was a lot longer these days. When breeding season was in full swing, however, she was dedicated and didn't like to waste a moment.

Their father dropped his napkin onto the table, leaned back in his chair, and smiled. Her sisters had inherited his red hair and stubborn temper. She took more after their deceased mom, with her blonde hair and tranquil exterior. Although she had to admit the McNeill temper hadn't skipped over her, hers just simmered instead of boiling over like Sam's or manifesting in mood swings like the artistic Dylan.

"So, I spoke to Harry and you won't believe this, but *Last Stop Durango* is already through edits and he wants an early Hollywood premiere." He grinned at all of them.

Amanda gazed at her sisters and Holt and they all shared varying versions of the same expression. From Sam's full jaw drop, to Dylan's wide eyes, to Holt's furrowed brow—shock to surprise. Harry Shaw was the old buddy of her father who'd brought the Western film to the ranch. For some reason, Amanda hadn't envisioned the final product of the filming from last summer. Apparently, neither did the rest of her family, except for her dad.

"Already? I thought it wasn't out until next

year?" Sam's voice rose.

This announcement was why he'd called them to lunch? Seriously? A pit formed in Amanda's belly. She and her sisters hadn't set foot in Los Angeles in over a dozen years. After the hell the paparazzi put them through after her mom's accident, she'd sworn to avoid it forever.

"Actually, it will be out this spring, believe it or not. And we've all been ordered to be there." Her dad kept the smile pasted on his face.

"Chris, tell them the rest of it." Angela laid a hand on his forearm.

"Well, I want us all to go as a family. A celebration of my part-time return to directing and a nod to Holt's hard work." Holt had been the stuntman for the lead actor, his final gig before retiring and starting his own stunt agency.

Nobody spoke. Amanda's fatigued brain worked to balance her dad's excitement with her sheer horror of returning to L.A. and the red carpet. Dylan and Sam wore identical frowns, which mirrored her own emotion.

Holt broke the tense silence. "I think it would great to come full circle with everything from last summer. That movie changed my life because it brought me here to my incredible wife." He grasped Sam's hand and leaned down to kiss their intertwined fingers.

Amanda watched her baby sister and her husband. Nobody could have predicted Sam, the resident tomboy, would fall in love and find marital bliss first. Holt and Sam were madly in love, even though they'd disliked each other on sight. Now, Amanda couldn't picture them not together––they were perfectly matched.

Amanda hadn't ever imagined her own wedding or even who would be the right man for her. After last night, Jake was definitely Mr. Right Now. And the present moment was her priority.

Sam smiled at him and looked around. "Holt has a point. It was tough to have everything from our past churned up, but we're all in a better place now, right? Maybe going to see the movie in L.A. would be a clean way to come full circle and let go of our issues from Hollywood for good."

Dylan shook her head. "I know it was great for you guys and I'm happy for you. You should go and cheer on Holt and dad. I'd rather skip it, if that's okay with everyone."

"Dylan, I'd love for us to do this as a family. It would mean a lot to me to have you all there. It was the first movie I helped direct in a dozen years. It was a turning point for me." His thick brows drew together.

Amanda sighed. "I'd really rather not go either. But..." She looked around and caught Dylan's eye. "But I agree it's important. Like a milestone or marker. Last summer was the beginning of getting closure and this could be another step. I'll go if you go, Dylan."

Dylan frowned at her and swung her gaze back to their dad. "I'll go on one condition."

Chris's brows rose.

"I still hate Hollywood and the paparazzi so,

can we just go up for the premiere, but not stay in L.A.? Or if you guys want to stay, you're okay with me coming home afterwards?"

"I second that motion. Plus I need to get home because of breeding season." Sam said.

Chris nodded. "Of course. I figured we could get a limo and go in style. They can just take us home after the screening."

"Or if your dad and I decide to stay over to celebrate, whoever wants to come back can take the car. Deal?" Angela gazed around the table.

Amanda was glad her stepmom seemed at peace with her dad returning part-time to his prior career. He'd given it all up for the family to be able to start over. Despite loving the ranch, the movie business flowed in his veins and now he could have the best of both worlds. Amanda wanted to support him.

"I'm in. Do you know what day yet?" And would Jake be her date for the premiere or would they still be seeing each other in secret? Or had last night been a one-time thing? She had no clue.

Her dad shook his head. "Not yet, but Harry's trying to pull some strings and confirm something next month."

"Wow, that seems so soon." Dylan gazed down at her plate. "But okay, I'll go."

"Thanks, honey. You don't know how much it means to me to have all my family with me for this." He beamed around the table.

Amanda hid another yawn behind her hand. Time to scoot back to the lab, where she could be alone and disguise her exhaustion. She pushed her chair back from the table.

"Oh, wait, one more thing. Do we officially have a new McNeill dog, Amanda?" Sam asked. "I'm getting attached to this sweetheart."

Stella was resting her chin on her sister's leg, looking quite pleased with herself.

Amanda hesitated and rose. "I haven't had that discussion with Jake yet."

"Sam, we have Stella most of the time already. I think it's sweet Jake wants to share custody with us. I mean he is the one who rescued her, right Amanda?" Dylan chimed in.

"Exactly. We've got Stella now, so let's just enjoy her and not make anything formal, okay? I've got to head back to the lab. Sam, you coming with?" Amanda carried her plate to the sink before anybody could commandeer it for her.

When she'd left Jake's this morning, Stella's joint custody was just a given. Why did her family need to have the answers now? She swallowed the prickle of irritation in her throat and summoned calm.

Her sister kissed Holt and stood up. "I'll be down in a couple minutes. I need to check something in the office up here first."

"See you all later." Amanda headed out, grateful to get back to the lab where she could replay last night in private. Again.

Would it be appropriate to ask Mr. Right Now to be her date to the premiere? Strolling back into the world that caused so much pain for her family would certainly be easier with Jake's stoic strength beside her. Or would she be blurring the lines between their private affair and a public relationship?

# CHAPTER 17

AMANDA CHECKED HER WATCH AGAIN. Only two more hours until she was meeting Jake to run stairs at the beach and to celebrate because he'd passed his sociology exam the second time around. Not just passed, but gotten a B+. Which simply proved her point he was absolutely capable of succeeding at work, studying for school, and sexy times with her.

Amanda leaned back in the office chair and shut out the vision of the charts on the computer screen and allowed herself to daydream. Almost a week since she'd kissed Jake goodbye after their magical night. A night that made her mind race and her heart flutter. Almost a week full of flirtatious text messages and mounting anticipation.

In a matter of a few weeks, her life looked and felt transformed. Where she'd been suffering from general malaise, now lightness characterized her mood. Instead of her usual hectic breeding season schedule, she was only working part-time. Instead of falling asleep with a book each night, she was sharing the bed with a gorgeous stud muffin. Well, with any luck she'd be sharing his bed again tonight. Touching him again. Feeling cherished and adored.

She smiled and massaged her upper arms. Grimaced when her tender left triceps reminded her of just why she was sitting on her butt in the office and not down checking on the mares. Letting go of control wasn't easy. Control was her middle name and if she'd learned anything in the last few weeks it was she actually didn't have control over anything external. All she could control were her own reactions to what was happening around her.

And with work, she was doing a spectacular job of not meddling, if she did say so herself. Not that she was currently checking Leo's work on a Sunday morning. Much as she hated to admit it, and she wouldn't admit it to anybody else, Leo was doing a good job handling her vet duties.

Well, an adequate job. She and Sam had perfected and implemented a flawless system over the years. Honed it to perfection. And he was using a totally different system. Her fingers itched to rearrange everything, but she would suck it up and watch from a distance.

With her recovery, she'd obeyed the physical therapist's directions, despite being certain she could perform the exercises at home without twice-weekly office visits. No way would she last six full weeks. Why was she even paying for physical therapy when she and Jake were working out this afternoon?

The only place where releasing control wasn't a challenge was with Jake. She shivered, imagining those strong, tanned hands holding and caressing her. In his arms, she could relinquish control. She was free to surrender, to let go, and to allow him to take the reins.

His powerful touch and skills in the bedroom rocked her beyond just the physical. He'd been so careful of her injuries, and so attentive to her pleasure. Beyond the multiple orgasms and sheer passion. He simultaneously made her feel protected and enflamed. She couldn't wait to see him this afternoon.

She smoothed her hands down her new fire-engine red, super-soft yoga pants. Why not splurge and get something she felt confident in? The pants and white tank just happened to match the white and red polka dot thong panties. And wasn't it fun to wear underwear somebody else would appreciate. Red was the color of passion and she hoped that's where the afternoon and dinner celebration would lead.

Her phone pinged. She picked it up and smiled when Jake's name appeared on the display. *Can't wait to see you. Don't forget Stella!*

*Me too. I couldn't stop her from coming if I tried. See you soon.* She sighed in relief their rendez-vous wouldn't be postponed again.

A few days earlier, she'd had to cancel their plans when Sam needed her in the lab. Because she hadn't felt truly needed since the Cowgirl incident, she couldn't refuse. At least now she wasn't working her regular breeding season schedule when she was basically on call around-the-clock.

In reality, their careers weren't particularly com-patible.

Jake had warned her of the volatility of his schedule. Well, the volatility of his entire career, actually. Although about eighty-five percent of the work he did was on medical calls, at any given time he could be called in for a fire. Of course on an intellectual level, she knew he had an incred-ibly dangerous career. But she hadn't allowed her mind to ponder the nitty-gritty details.

Jake tilted his face up so the full force of the icy spray blasted his face. Prayed the freezing water would wake him up. He'd slept like crap at the station and drank gallons of coffee this morning to power through another study session. Although he wanted to see Amanda, he had zero energy and running stairs and motivating her to do the same held little appeal. Flopping on the couch in front of the TV sounded like heaven. Damn it.

Almost a whole week had elapsed since she'd left his apartment, rumpled and satisfied. No way would he risk disappointing her, but a nap sounded ideal. He switched off the shower. He was just pulling on a pair of sweats when the door-bell rang. He hurried to the door and whipped it open. And just like that, his shitty attitude disap-peared.

Stella trotted toward him, her tail wagging like mad. When he caught sight of Amanda, his eyes almost rolled backwards in his head. Snug red leggings hugged her slender thighs and gently curving hips. A fitted white fleece jacket high-lighted her shape and framed her face.

Bam. He was wide awake.

"Hello, handsome." She stepped into his arms and he pulled her into his naked torso. Goosebumps erupted all over his body when she stroked her slender hands up his bare back.

"Cold?" She murmured against his chest.

He tilted his head back and gazed down into her feline green eyes. "Not even close." He captured her mouth with his and groaned when her soft lips parted for him immediately. Her warm breath tasted of mint. Her fingernails dug into his skin and her body melted into him, plastering them together from shoulder to toes.

Stella barked, apparently disgruntled at not receiving an immediate embrace too. Jake laughed, feeling sunnier than he had since he'd seen Amanda last.

He stepped back and crouched down to hug the dog. "Sorry, girl, feeling left out?"

Amanda chuckled. "Stella missed you too. But don't feel too bad; she gets constant attention, twenty-four-seven. She's a spoiled girl."

He gazed up at her. Damn she was beautiful. "I've missed you both. What a week."

She stroked her fingers through his hair and he pushed his head against her hand. Kind of like the dog. "You look sleepy. Do you want to skip the stairs today and go straight out to dinner?"

He purred under her attention and every muscle

in his body stirred to attention. He rose to his feet and captured her hands in his. "No, let's do it if you're feeling up to it. I want to hold up my end of our bargain." *Although I'd rather get you naked right now.*

She bit her full lower lip and nodded, the early afternoon sunlight streaming in from the living room windows dancing off the varied shades of gold in her silky hair. "The more consistent I am with my workouts, the sooner I'll be back to normal. And Stella would be disappointed. Let's do it. I'm treating you to dinner afterwards. I found a great spot where Stella can hang with us on a heated patio."

"You don't have to do that––I'm going to be taking a lot of tests." Jake smiled and fetched a shirt and his jacket. The sooner they left, the sooner they could return to his place.

"I know, but this one feels symbolic somehow. Please, I want to celebrate. Okay?" She threaded her fingers through his and squeezed.

"Let's do this." They left the apartment and set out for his favorite set of steep wooden stairs at Swami's State Beach.

Stella threw herself down at the base of the steps, her breath coming in sharp pants. Amanda cradled her left arm and couldn't hide a grimace of pain. Jake's calves were burning, but he'd planned on them running ten cycles of sprints. After five rounds, he would be happy to throw in the towel and grab some dinner.

"Why don't we call it a day? We don't want to push Stella too far." *And I don't want to push you too far either.*

"I'm fine. We can wrap her leash around the post and she can wait for us. I don't want to quit." Sweat beaded across Amanda's brow and determination glinted in her emerald eyes.

"Look, you're just a few weeks out from a serious injury. Why don't we just stretch and head to dinner? I'm starving." *And you look like you just ran a marathon.*

Amanda shook her head. "I'm fine. I need to do this, Jake. Come on." She started up the stairs and he had no choice but to follow after loosely tying Stella's leash to the post. Damn, she was stubborn.

She was halfway up the second set of stairs when she slipped on the wet, sandy wood. She caught herself on the railing, but couldn't prevent the cry of pain.

"Amanda." He came up behind her and wrapped her gently into his arms. "I can tell you're hurting. Don't push yourself. I want you to heal up fast too, but if you overdo it, you might delay your recovery."

She blew out a breath. "This stinks. I should be able to do all these sprints, no problem. But you're right. My shoulder's killing me." She dropped her forehead against his chest.

He stroked one hand down her back and cupped the back of her head with the other. "Look at me."

She tilted her head up and he captured her

mouth with his. Her soft lips parted for him and her arms wrapped around his waist. He pulled her in close, savoring her sweet breath and the mingling of the ocean air and her unique beachy scent. A seagull squawked and yanked him from the trance of being in her arms.

He laughed. "Let's get Stella and go home."

She pouted. "But I want to take you to dinner. We're supposed to be celebrating your awesome grade."

"We can do it another night. Right now, I want to drive you back to my place and take care of you." He'd rather have her in his arms and on his couch, than be out in public.

She sighed. "If you're sure. But you aren't getting out of it. At least I can order us take out, okay?"

He smiled and brushed a loose strand of silky hair away from her forehead. "Deal."

Once they returned to his apartment, they crossed straight to the couch he'd been fantasizing about earlier and sank into the cushions together. The reality of pulling her onto his lap, of enfolding her in his arms, obliterated his earlier intention to tend to her injuries.

"Let me get you some ice and some ibuprofen." He struggled to resist the urge to make love to her and to act like a good guy.

In response, she snuggled closer and the press of her tight little butt in his lap jolted him to full attention. She brushed her lips along his neck, and lightning sparked across his skin. She continued biting and kissing his neck and his head fell back along the couch. Amanda shifted and straddled him, and the heat of her center rocked against his erection.

"Amanda, you're hurt." His protest was weak in his own ears.

"I know what will make me feel better," she whispered, her voice husky and sexy as hell.

His arms banded around her, crushing her against his chest. Why was she still wearing a fleece jacket? He leaned her back and yanked the zipper down. She shrugged the coat off and revealed her satiny skin and a thin tank top. He slid his hands up from her waist to cover her breasts, brushing her rosy nipples with his thumbs until they tightened against his palms.

He slid the tank top off, careful around her left shoulder. The bruises were turning yellow, but still reminded him of her vulnerability. Once she was as bare as he was, he pulled her in closer. Her weight sank against his and he groaned. She fit perfectly against him, her soft breasts smashed against his chest, her fingers digging into his hair, her mouth fused to his.

Well, he did want to make her feel better——he'd hate to disappoint her. He wrapped his hands around her hips and lifted her to the side.

"No, where are you going? " she murmured.

He kissed her again and slid her soft red yoga pants down and growled when he saw her red polka-dot underwear. "Are you trying to kill me? These are sexy as hell."

She raised a brow. "You like? I bought them for you."

He gently pressed her back against the pillows, and took off the scrap of material. "Oh yeah, I like them. Are you okay like this?"

"Mmmm…yes, I want to feel your weight on me. And you inside me. Now please." She reached up and clasped his hips.

He braced his forearms on the cushions to protect her. "Your wish is my command. Wrap your legs around me."

He groaned when her satin skin squeezed around his waist and he slid home.

Amanda cracked open one eye and was greeted by a smooth bronze expanse of chiseled pecs and ridged abs. She popped open the other eye and struggled to orient herself. Where was she?

Jake's apartment. Jake's couch. Jake's carved-from-marble body cradling hers in his arms. When she tilted her head back, she paused to admire his relaxed jaw and sweep of heavy black lashes. He was fast asleep, his breath steady and even, like the rise and fall of his chest.

Unfortunately, she needed to use the bathroom and couldn't wait another second. She eased herself off the couch, lifting one heavy arm and gently releasing it. He didn't budge. Just how much sleep did he actually get at the fire station?

She hurried to the bathroom and stifled a scream at the woman in the mirror sporting a wild straw mop on her head. Yes, their sexual chemistry was off the charts electric, but she looked like she'd actually been electrocuted. She washed her face and used Jake's wide-toothed comb to restore some semblance of order to her hair.

When she returned to the living room, Jake had settled onto his back on the jumbo-sized dark couch and snored quietly. Stella snoozed in her bed close by. The clock over the large gas range alerted her they'd napped for more than two hours. Or at least they'd returned more than two hours ago. Her lips curved up and she ran her fingertips along her swollen, tender lips. Jake was the most incredible kisser she'd ever encountered. An incredible lover.

Her stomach growled. They'd never gotten around to ordering takeout. Jake had to be hungry when he woke up too, right? Maybe Jake had some of his father's cooking again. She crossed to the refrigerator and poked around the shelves. A casserole dish containing something delicious looking appeared promising for an early dinner. She placed it on the counter and debated between the oven and the microwave.

"According to my dad, it's better heated up in the oven. The microwave will make it rubbery." Jake slid his arms around her and pulled her naked back against his front.

Amanda leaned her head back and savored the feel of his solid body embracing her. She hugged his arms closer to her and smiled. "The oven it is. I'd love some wine if you've got it."

He turned her to face him and pressed a light kiss against her mouth. "Let me grab some pants and we'll put it all together."

"If you have to…" She smiled at him, unable to get her fill of his magnificent physique. "I guess I'll put my pants on too."

"Do you want a t-shirt or sweatshirt?"

The idea of snuggling into his clothes sounded like a lovely idea. "That would be great. I'll turn on the oven. Three fifty okay?" Not that she was much of a cook, but she could warm up leftovers.

He returned with a bottle of ibuprofen and a Pink Floyd t-shirt. He helped her slide it on over her shoulder, his touch gentle. When the hem brushed her knees, she twirled around.

"I don't suppose you have a belt for this?" She laughed.

He grinned, his strong white teeth flashing in his bronzed face. "The belt would be too big too, sorry."

Once the chicken enchiladas were hot, they took plates and wineglasses to snuggle on the overstuffed couch. Amanda sipped the nice red blend from Sonoma. His sweet concern and his tenderness warmed her from within. When had she felt so safe and content? As if everything in the world was fine, as long as they could hang out doing simple things, like savoring the normalcy of eating leftovers in front of the television.

"I feel awful. Here I was going to treat you for kicking butt on your test and you're actually pampering me and I'm eating your leftovers." She frowned.

He took her empty plate and placed it on the coffee table next to his. "Don't you get it? I'm loving this celebration. I've got you all to myself and my dad's cooking is the best. You even cleaned your plate."

Amanda laughed. She never cleaned her plate. "Well, you worked me hard this afternoon. I built up an appetite." And she wasn't referring to the stair workout.

"Not too hard?" His dark brows knit together.

She stroked her fingertips along his forehead, smoothing the crease. "Everything was perfect. I'm not as delicate as I look."

He smiled and snuggled her in closer to him. "Do you feel like watching a movie?" He murmured the words against her neck, his firm lips brushing the sensitive skin below her ear.

She shivered. "Sounds perfect. Do you like old movies?"

He nibbled down her neck to press kisses along her collarbone. "Like how old? The eighties?"

Amanda laughed, recalling the twins' comment about she and Jake's meeting again  was like a 1980s romcom. "I was thinking black and white, but an 80s classic works too."

"You are older than me, maybe we see that differently." He sat back with a smile, and a shallow dimple appeared in his right cheek.

"Very funny. Not that much older. A couple of my favorites were *Ferris Bueller's Day Off* or *The Lost Boys.*"

"I loved *The Lost Boys* and it's been forever. Let's see if we can get it." He grabbed one of the four remote controls on his teak coffee table and flicked on the television. Scrolling through the listings at a terrifying speed, he found the movie in about thirty seconds. "And here you go. You ready?"

She nodded, set her half-empty wine glass on the table, and nestled in closer to him. "Absolutely."

A few enjoyable hours later, he flicked off the TV.

He scooped her into his arms and deposited her on his enormous bed. She could get used to him carrying her to bed. He lay down next to her, turned her on her right side, and snuggled her in close. With his arms wrapped around her waist and her head tucked onto his broad shoulder, they fit like two puzzle pieces. Amanda's last waking thought was she couldn't remember ever being happier.

# CHAPTER 18

A MANDA SPRANG UP, HER HEAD whipping side-to-side, trying to identify the source of the horrific noise assaulting her ears. Adrenaline shot through her veins and her heart pounded. The clock on the nightstand next to her read 3:02. Was Jake's smoke alarm going off or were those sirens wailing around his apartment complex?

Jake leapt out of bed and yanked on pants. "Sorry, that's my special ring for work. Emergency call. Fire out near Fairbanks Ranch." He pulled a t-shirt over his head.

Amanda rubbed the grittiness out of her eyes. "I thought you were off? Aren't other people working tonight?" He'd just finished extra long hours at the station.

"Emergency. Everyone has to show up, on duty or off. Sorry, gotta run and don't know when I'll be back. Please lock the door when you leave." He kissed her distractedly on the forehead and before she could respond, the front door slammed behind him.

Amanda sat frozen in the bed. It was three o'clock in the morning and now she was wide awake. What was she supposed to do? It wasn't like she was going to get up and drive home now. Nor was it likely she could fall back asleep after such a harsh awakening.

Maybe Stella wanted to snuggle. She patted the bed; Stella trotted into the room and leapt up. She settled the animal onto the blankets and hugged her close. "It's just you and me, girl. Let's take a little nap."

Despite the comfort of spooning the warm fuzzy dog, Amanda tossed and turned, unable to fall back asleep. Being in Jake's apartment without him felt strangely intimate. Too intimate after only staying over a few times. Her stomach churned and she pressed her hands against her belly. Her eyes flew open and she stared at the ceiling, any pretense of sleep gone.

He hadn't rushed out his apartment for a drill: there was a fire in Rancho Santa Fe. She sat up, her heart racing. Every time he went on a call could potentially be the last time. On an intellectual level, she'd recognized it, but now the reality punched her in the chest. Although he'd claimed most of his time was spent responding to emergency medical calls and accidents, the fact was fifteen percent of his time was devoted to fighting fires.

And he planned on spending his entire career as a firefighter, whether he was promoted to captain or not. Could she handle the not knowing what was happening every single time? Her stomach pitched and rolled.

Bile rose in Amanda's throat. Unlike her sister Sam, who had been on set the day their mom died, Amanda had been at the library studying, alone. Like she always had during high school—getting into a top university and veterinary school required perfect grades. Her studies came first, no matter what. One of her father's staff, Craig Wynter, had found her tucked into a carrel in the library stacks. At first, she thought she'd simply lost track of time and Craig was picking her up for an important family dinner or event.

Her mom's job shouldn't have been dangerous. After all, she had been a dramatic actress, not an action star. Usually, she'd had a stunt person stand in on any of the movie scenes considered precarious. But one day, she'd insisted she didn't need a stand-in for a relatively innocuous scene and it was the last decision she'd made. A freak accident altered the fates of the McNeill family forever.

When she'd looked at Craig's face and truly seen his stricken expression, a buzzing had started in her ears, ice slicked over her skin, and her legs hadn't wanted to support her when she'd tried to stand. The musty scent of old books and lemon wood polish had always comforted her before, but from that day forward, Amanda hadn't been able to study in isolated desks close to old books. The smell literally made her want to vomit.

Craig wouldn't explain what happened, just kept repeating he had to get her to her dad and he'd explain everything. She'd been screaming inside her head, but was too polite and too numb to actually vocalize her fear. He'd driven her to her house, where her dad and sisters were huddled on the crushed velvet navy couch. Sam and Dylan's faces wore identical expressions of devastation, their chocolate brown eyes swimming in tears, their usually smiling mouths downturned. Her father's face had been pasty white when he'd simply reached out a hand for her to join them.

After the initial shock wore off, numbness became Amanda's default. The only way she could cope with the funeral and then the paparazzi nightmare swirling around her mom's death. How she compartmentalized her mom never returning home from work one day.

Numbness shifted into responsibility. She'd been a senior in high school and her sisters had only been fifteen years old. Once they'd moved to Pacific Vista Ranch, Amanda continued to focus on her studies, but also took special care to look out for her sisters. Luckily Angela entered their lives, first as the household manager, and then as their stepmom.

And so Amanda had found it easier to be the independent one, the one who didn't rely on anyone, the one who was so capable she could deal with any situation herself. Of course her dad had been protective and supportive. But from that day forward, she avoided forming many close attachments because the raw pain of losing her beloved mother had ripped an irreparable tear in her heart. Avoided putting herself in any situation where she'd be left waiting and wondering. Her family and work on the ranch were safe.

Every hour she spent with Jake deepened her feelings for him. Their relationship was progressing at a rapid pace and growing more serious by the moment. She drew in a long inhale and held her breath. Sighed it out. She pressed her hand against her pounding heart and fell back against the pillows. She was already half in love with him.

Now she was recognizing just how dangerous those tender feelings were. What if he went to work and didn't come home? Would one of his co-workers wearing a compassionate expression come find her at the ranch, just like Craig had come to find her when her mom died? A shiver racked through her. How had she allowed this to happen?

On top of the life or death risks he took regularly, his job would always take precedence. How could she or any woman ever be his number one priority? Of course, she was independent and accustomed to taking care of herself, but she did want to be someone's number one. Jake's protectiveness and strength had filled her with happiness because he always seemed to have her back. As if he'd always be there to take care of her if she needed it. Like he'd done when he'd found her on the ground after Cowgirl kicked her.

An urgent need to flee filled her, despite the pre-dawn hour. No matter how much she attempted to slow her breathing down, her heart continued to thunder like she was sprinting to win a race. She dressed and drove back to the ranch with

Stella. Maybe once she got home, she could find a way to process her newly recognized feelings.

And the fear skittering down her spine.

# CHAPTER 19

JAKE SCRUTINIZED THE DARK SMOKE-FILLED cul-de-sac, working to get his bearings now the fire truck had pulled up to the subdivision. A towering blaze billowed flames and smoke. Another truck from the station had arrived first and guys were focusing on what appeared to be a few houses at the end of the street. Nothing else seemed to be burning.

Yet.

Although they hadn't identified where the fire had started, flames licked around a few houses at the far end of the street and in the scrubby chaparral covered hillsides behind it.

Homeowners were under strict orders to comply with landscaping rules governing certain types of trees and even the proper spacing of mulch from the houses.

Jake hoped like hell this neighborhood was in compliance.

Everything could amplify in minutes.

The captain radioed to hit the steep hillsides on the east side of the subdivision to ensure the embers were extinguished. Otherwise, they could blow out onto a wood roof or a leaf-filled gutter. If they could stop the houses from catching fire and the flames from spreading, they could have the blaze handled. The priority was saving the homes and people.

After the Witch Creek fire in 2007 where homes were lost, Rancho Santa Fe had to make changes to protect the people. The whole covenant was a potential disaster area. Many of the newer homes in the neighborhood had been built with noncombustible roofs and siding, but many of the homes weren't new. With the other guys working on the houses, Jake and his team focused on ensuring the vegetation was clear of any embers or flames. To ensure not just this neighborhood was clear, but that the fire didn't leap over any of the canyons and tree-filled spaces.

Between the coordinated attacks, the team was able to knock the fire down in less than an hour. Jake trudged back to the truck and his buddy Parks handed him a bottle of water. He grabbed the drink and chugged all sixteen ounces in one shot. Sweat dripped into his eyes and he swiped his brow.

"Not sure why all us off-duty guys had to come for this call, are you?" Parks grimaced. "Don't know about you, but I was off in dreamland."

Jake's brain immediately switched from work to the soft, beautiful woman he'd left in his bed. Leaving her had been tough in more ways than one. He was still wiped out from his shift, but more importantly, he'd hated leaving her alone.

"Yeah, not ideal."

Parks pointed toward the entrance to the cul-de-sac. "Did you see the News trucks down the street? Is this a celebrity's house or something?"

Jake looked around and noticed the van for the first time. "No clue, man. I mean all these houses are worth millions. Maybe there was arson or something?"

Parks shrugged and shook his head.

"Guys, get back to the station. Quick meeting." Moyer barked across the asphalt at them.

Jake groaned and muttered to Parks. "Seriously? And why is he the one shouting orders?"

Parks frowned. "Let's go. The sooner we get back, the sooner we can get home."

They skirted around the news crew, loaded up, and drove back to their station. After everybody finished their routines, they gathered around the meeting table. Captain Roberts explained why everyone had been called for this fire. Apparently, after the major scare last summer when Jake had checked in at Pacific Vista Ranch, the department wasn't taking any chances of acceleration.

California had had tough fire seasons over the last few years and San Diego County didn't want to become a statistic like Napa Valley or L.A. or risk a replay of the Witch Creek fire. The wealthy citizens of Rancho Santa Fe were influential and after homes were lost in past fires, the department had been directed to treat each fire like it could potentially be a major disaster. Despite the relatively minor nature of the fire tonight, it was clear these calls could become more of a rule than the exception.

Sunlight streamed through the windows of the team lounge. Jake massaged the tightness at the back of his neck. The three a.m. calls never got easier. But if Amanda was still warming his bed when he returned home, maybe he could salvage some of this morning. Leaving her had been tough and reminded him of one of the reasons he'd not been in a hurry to get seriously involved with a woman.

Several of the members of his team were married, but he'd always wondered if it was smart to put down ties. Was the risk worth it to leave their partner widowed? The more time he spent with Amanda, the more tempting it was to make plans for the future. Although, she'd only noticed him a few weeks ago, and he'd put her on a pedestal twelve years ago. For all he knew, commitment wasn't on her mind.

He grabbed his backpack to check if Amanda had texted. When he opened the bag, his stack of flash cards spilled out all over the locker room floor. *Damn it.* He hissed out a breath and he looked around to make sure he was still alone.

He exhaled unsteadily, crouched down, and gathered up the cards. The last thing he needed was for someone to clue in to his studying.

He scanned the floor and spotted one last card, which had somehow blown almost to the doorway and rose from his hands and knees to fetch it.

And there was Moyer in the doorway, one steel-toed boot planted on the card. "Is this what you're crawling around the floor for?"

Jake ground his teeth and fought to come up with a swift reply. Due to his long shift, last night's incredible sex, and the rude wake up call at three a.m., quick wasn't exactly how his brain was functioning.

"Just hand it over."

Moyer's bushy red brows rose. "We'll see what it is first." He bent over and snatched up the card before Jake could beat him to it.

Like he could rip it out from under the guy's shoe.

"Huh, survival of the fittest as a sociologic norm." Moyer narrowed his eyes at Jake.

"Just hand it over."

Moyer snickered and handed him the card. Jake's jaw almost dropped, but he clicked it shut. The guy was just going to give it back without further harassment? Unbelievable. Jake tucked the card back into his notebook, intent on getting out of there without any further confrontation.

Moyer leaned back against the doorjamb, forcing Jake to have to turn sideways to get out the door. When he was almost through, Moyer said, "Looks like someone thinks they'll beat me out for captain in a few years. The odds of you getting a college degree are like the Buffalo Bills ever winning a Super Bowl."

"Screw you, Moyer." Jake cleared the doorway. Ignoring the prick was the only way to handle this, even though he wanted to punch the sneer off his pasty freckled face.

"Even animals with brains the size of peas can have quick reaction times and tons of muscle. Doesn't make them smart enough to lead a crew. Why put yourself through the stress of trying to get a degree? It won't matter anyway."

Jake froze, his hands curling into fists. Every single laugh, every single joke made at his expense when he was a kid, every shove he'd gotten in the school hallways jolted into his system. Like it was yesterday.

*Jake's not smart enough. Not fast enough. Not enough.*

He fought to control his breathing. He'd never have a shot at captain if he rose to the jerk's pathetic attempt to draw him into a fight. Without turning around, he bit out, "Must be worried, Moyer, or why would you care what I do?"

With the echoes of Moyer's laughter in his ears, Jake forced himself to saunter out of the station. He reached his truck, climbed inside, and accelerated out of the lot. He gripped the steering wheel and regulated his breathing. After a few minutes, his shoulders relaxed. He would shrug it off. Moyer's crap had nothing to do with him and the guy thrived on shoveling reams of it to everyone at the station.

Jake's phone rang and his dad's name flashed up on the dashboard screen. He frowned. Why would his dad be calling him at 6:30 in the morning?

His fingers tightened on the steering wheel. "Hey, dad, everything okay?"

"Morning, Jake. Everything is great. Are you okay? You must be feeling tired." His dad's voice was animated and he wasn't usually a morning person

"I am, but what's with the early call?"

"Your mother and I were having our first cups of coffee and watching the news this morning. They were calling you and your crew heroes for handling that fire in the middle of the night so fast."

"Me? Or our station?"

"They actually mentioned your name as the driver of the fire truck. We were hoping they were going to interview you."

Jake shuddered. Thank god they hadn't. Like he'd have anything insightful to say. "Just doing my job, Dad. We go out on calls all the time. Not sure why this one warranted a news story."

"That's why I called." His father's voice grew serious.

Jake waited for him to continue.

"You still there?"

"Yeah, Dad. So what's up?" His dad didn't usually prevaricate.

His dad exhaled. "Seeing you guys in action and seeing what you do every day, I just wanted to call you and tell you I am proud of you."

Jake's foot jerked on the pedal and he caught himself before he ran the stop sign. Barely.

Proud of him? His dad? "Um, thanks."

"Your mom pointed out to me that I make too big of a deal about Rafe's work and not enough about yours. And it hit me like a ton of bricks this morning. I'm sorry if I don't tell you enough that I think you're a modern day superhero."

Jake parked his truck in his apartment complex's reserved spot and turned off the engine. Was he dreaming? He glanced at the display again and sure enough, his dad's number was on it.

"Dad, I don't know what to say." His parents had told him they were proud of him, but his dad's admission blew him away. Apologizing for not calling him a superhero?

"No need to say anything. I know we don't do big talks or anything. But I recognized I was doing to you what my parents did to me when I chose culinary school over college. And that messed with my head for a long time, no matter how successful I've been." He paused and audibly swallowed. "I am proud of you and what you do."

Jake stared out the window, his mind whirling. Was all of his motivation to get a degree and become captain based on his dad's approval or was it what he wanted for himself? Releasing the crushing pressure of studying and written exams would be a welcome relief. Not beating himself up for wanting to just date Amanda without tutoring would make his life simpler.

"Jake?"

"Sorry, Dad, like I said, I'm tired and this phone call is out of the blue." And now I'm not sure what to do or what I want if I'm not being driven by a misguided desire to make you proud of me.

"Go take a nap. You deserve it. And Jake?" His

father's voice held a hint of doubt.

"Yeah?"

"I love you."

Jake's chest tightened. This might have been the most personal discussion between he and his dad, ever. "I love you too, Dad."

After they hung up, Jake sat in the car. Floored.

He had some serious thinking to do. About school. About being a captain. And about Amanda. Although he'd defied his gut instinct that he should either have her as his tutor or his lover, he couldn't ignore the niggling doubt in the back of his brain.

Although she didn't seem to mind combining their bargain and a personal relationship, he did. She appeared content to go on hikes and work out and hang out at his place. While every time he saw her or, hell, every time they texted, deeper feelings were surfacing. Visions of something more than friends with benefits. The quiet night they'd stayed in and watched old movies had given him a glimpse of what life could be like—a perfect balance to both of their hectic careers.

Sure, they were having a good time and their chemistry was off the charts. But he wanted more. His childhood crush didn't compare to the real experience of being Amanda's man. He didn't want to be simply the guy who helped her get out of what she called her "rut."

And he wasn't going to just be a booty call.

Hell, he was falling in love with her. For real. Not the immature boy's fantasy of who he imagined Amanda to be. Now they'd been together, he could picture her as his partner, the mother of his children, as the one for him. Could she picture him as her life partner?

And why the hell couldn't he just figure out what was good enough for him and stop worrying about how everyone else saw him?

He yanked open the door and stepped out of the car. He had a wild pack of monkeys zooming around in his brain. What he needed was a long run to clear his head.

Today might be a day that could change everything. Forever.

# CHAPTER 20

AFTER AMANDA SNEAKED BACK INTO the dark house with Stella, she thanked the universe she'd gotten home before anyone was stirring. She settled Stella in her dog bed in the kitchen and climbed the stairs to her bedroom. She ached. Her shoulder alternated between sharp shooting pains and a dull throb. The rest of her body throbbed from yet another passionate lovemaking session with Jake. Her heart? No clue.

She strolled into her bathroom, turned the shower on, and dialed it up to scalding hot. Immediately, misty tendrils clouded the glass shower walls. Amanda peeled off her clothes and placed them into the sleek hamper against the far wall of the spacious room. When she stepped into the steaming hot water, she hissed when the strong pressure hit her left side, which was still a watercolor of fading purples and yellows and greens. She shifted so the spray peppered her back and head directly, savoring the intensity.

Jake's swift exit had chilled her. She'd reverted to her old set point of numb, and perhaps here in the bliss of her shower and the privacy of pre-dawn, she could sort through what she was feeling. She scratched her fingernails into her scalp as she massaged shampoo through her hair. Smiled remembering raking them down Jake's broad muscular back.

Her temples pounded, probably from the crappy night's sleep and the rude awakening. The water soothed her, but caffeine called. She flicked off the water and dressed in her favorite faded jeans and surprise, surprise, her green zip-up hoodie. She'd have to burn the thing in a few weeks after wearing it as her daily uniform.

She checked her phone, but Jake hadn't texted. Combing her wet hair, she tucked it behind her ears and padded silently downstairs to see if anyone was up and making gallons of coffee or if she needed to brew a pot. With all the lab work she had in front of her, she'd need toothpicks to prop her eyelids open.

Although the house was still dark, a light filtered through the crack in the kitchen doorway. Booming voices and background racket made it sound like a party was happening in the kitchen at 6:30 a.m.

Her dad stood whistling at the industrial-sized coffee and espresso machine with Stella leaning against his legs. The television was blaring in the family room, which explained the noise.

So much for a peaceful start to the morning after last night's drama. Digging deep, she walked in and pasted on a smile. "You're up early."

Her dad turned and grinned, the grooves

around his mouth deepening. "There's my favorite daughter."

She relaxed and laughed. "You're incorrigible. I know you tell Sam and Dylan the same thing." *Please don't comment on how early I'm up.*

He pulled her in for a gentle hug. "You're all my favorites. Can I pour you some coffee? Make you something to eat?"

Her dad was definitely not famous for his cooking skills. "Just coffee, thanks."

He poured them both cups and they sat at the breakfast nook. "How's the shoulder? And how is Leo working out?"

She frowned. "My shoulder's healing. I really think everything will be fine soon. And Leo is doing a good job, although it kills me to admit that."

He laughed. "You got that from me———being a perfectionist is tough."

She nodded and laughed again, her mood lightening simply being in her dad's presence. "Right? The effort it takes not to go down to the barn or to the clinic and rearrange how he set things up? Killing me."

"It's just temporary. What else is new? I thought I'd be seeing you more while you recuperated, but it seems like less."

Amanda shrugged and angled her body toward the television. Had she heard something about fire? "Just busy with the therapy and some workouts and——Oh My God!" She jumped up from the chair. Stella barked and danced around her legs.

Her dad stood too and looked around. "What is it?"

She pointed at the TV and hurried closer to the screen. "Fire in Rancho Santa Fe." Her voice wavered.

A local reporter, bundled up, was speaking into the camera with billowing smoke creating a dramatic backdrop. Two or three fire trucks were parked behind her and firefighters in bright helmets and full-suited uniforms swarmed in the background at a full run. Because their faces were shrouded, Amanda couldn't determine if one of them was Jake.

Her father joined her, massaging her healthy shoulder. "This was from earlier, around three in the morning. They extinguished it pretty quickly. A few houses in Fairbanks Ranch and some of the hillside scrub brush. Nobody was hurt."

She whipped her head toward him. "Are you sure?"

He cocked his head, his hazel eyes narrowing. "Yes I'm sure. They're just re-running the clip again. Apparently the fire department wanted to make sure they caught it early and doubled up on crew to make sure nothing sparked and jumped any canyons or lit any trees."

Amanda exhaled an unsteady breath and held her hand to her heart. Jake was okay. She turned and returned to the table on trembling legs and sank into her seat. She grasped her cheerful flowered mug in both hands and sipped her coffee. She closed her eyes—Jake wasn't injured.

Her father slid into the booth next to her. "You okay?"

She nodded and kept her eyes on her drink. "Yeah, I just didn't get much sleep last night and I'm a little on edge."

"Is that why you rolled in so early this morning with Stella?" He asked quietly.

*Crap.* Her stomach dropped. "Dad, I'm an adult."

"I'm not judging or asking for details. It's just when you came home, Stella decided to come join Angela and me. Woke me up. Were you with the firefighter and he got called to the fire?"

Her dad was nothing if not astute. Not that it took a rocket scientist to know where she'd been with the "shared custody" dog. "Yes, he got an alarm or page or whatever at three in the morning. So to see it on the news just scared me. That's all." No way was she discussing her and Jake's relationship, but she wasn't going to lie either.

"Have you heard from him since?"

She cleared her throat and shook her head.

"Amanda, look at me." His baritone was gentle.

Reluctantly, she lifted her head and peered at him with raised brows.

"Is this thing serious with you and Jake?"

She shrugged. "It's only been a few weeks, Dad. He's the first man I've been interested in for years. He's a great guy and we're having fun. But, for some reason I don't think I really considered the realities of his job, you know?"

He covered her hand with his. "He does seem

like a great guy. I saw the way he looked at you and Sam mentioned you'd been his tutor back in high school?"

Amanda narrowed her eyes. Did everyone know this now? "Sam told you that?"

"Yes, we do talk about you. I know you haven't dated much and I've always worried about you holding yourself back that way."

"Worried about me? I thought—"

"I worry about everyone in my family, including you. You're one of the strongest women I know and I'm so proud of what you've done with your life so far. But I would love it if you found someone you love and could build a life with too. I don't know if it's this guy or not, but seeing you spending time with someone who so obviously adores you is a good thing."

Amanda nibbled on her lip. "So you don't think I can always take care of myself then?"

"Of course you can. But you don't always have to. And we're always here for you. Ever since your mom died, it seemed like you thought you had to take care of everyone. That's too much of a burden, Amanda." His hazel eyes shimmered with unshed tears.

"Dylan and Sam were so young and I know how devastated you were." She reached for his hand again.

"You were young too, Amanda. You're only two years older than them, not twenty. And we were all devastated. But things are changing and shifting, and if you like this guy…" He smiled and shrugged.

"But Dad, he fights fires. Every time he steps out the door could be his last. Casually seeing him is one thing, but I don't know if I can handle that on a long-term basis, you know? Tonight scared me. I still haven't heard from him."

Her dad's brows knit together. "And you were the last to know about your mom. You've got a point. But Sam was worried about Holt's stunt work. Granted, he's not doing it any longer, but you know a person's career is part of them. You can't ask someone to change that. You also can't live your life fearing something will happen. Your mom's accident was out of the blue. People get hit by cars. Get cancer. Have heart attacks. You never know."

"That's not morbid at all, Dad." Her lips curved up despite herself.

He squeezed her hands. "You know what I mean. Don't let fear hold you back."

"Don't let fear hold you back from what?" Dylan wandered into the kitchen.

"Nothing." Amanda rose from her chair. She needed to ponder everything, to dig into this maelstrom of emotions swirling through her. What she didn't need was her sweet, emotional little sister extending the conversation she was ready to finish with their dad.

Dylan enfolded her in a gentle hug. "Everything okay?"

"I'm fine. What are you doing up this early? I thought you never woke up before nine?" So much for having the house to herself while she drank her coffee and contemplated her situation with Jake.

Dylan shrugged, avoided her gaze, and crossed to the coffee maker. "Texting with one of my friends in France who forgot the time difference."

"You are *not* going to Paris again instead of staying for the premiere with the rest of us." No way was she going to let her little sister escape all the movie business again. If Amanda had to go, Dylan would too.

Dylan gasped. "No. Why would you think that?"

"Just making sure." Suddenly she remembered her dad was still in the room with them. "Sorry, Dad. But this has to be a whole family affair, right?"

Their dad frowned. "Do you girls really not want to go?"

Amanda and Dylan both shook their heads. "We're going. I think it's important we're all together though. Are our brothers coming and do we have a date yet?"

"Potentially in two or three weeks. Another film ran into some problems so, we might get their screening night. Nothing like last minute. Not sure about the guys. I doubt Grant could pull it off, but Angela was checking with Ryan and Austin."

"Yeah, they need to come too. And I guess we're shopping for dresses." Dylan's lips curved up.

Amanda smiled at her sister, who was the girly-girl in the family. "We should go together so you can help Sam and me. Well, we may just have to buy Sam's because I doubt we can drag her away from the horses."

"Yes, it will be fun. And hopefully your bruises will be gone by then."

Amanda grimaced. "They better be. Okay, I'm going to head up to the office and get to work. Have a good day in the studio, Dylan, and I'll see you later, Dad."

With a half wave, Amanda sauntered out the door. She was halfway down the hallway to her office when Dylan caught up with her. "Hey, wait up."

Amanda paused and sipped her coffee. "You going to come help me enter stats?"

Dylan smirked. "Right. I can't risk tiring these artistic fingers before I go back to the piece I'm working on."

"You've used that excuse for years, but I guess you're right. Something on your mind?" She didn't want to chase off her sister, but she was tired.

Dylan nodded. "Let's chat in the office."

They entered and Dylan pulled the brass-handled door shut behind them. Amanda plopped down in her comfy office chair, drew her legs underneath her, and raised her eyebrows.

Dylan sat down on one of the low-slung leather chairs facing her. "So, a couple things. What's going on with Jake? Are you inviting him to the premiere?"

Amanda hesitated. "I don't know."

"You don't know how things are or you don't know if you're going to invite him?"

"Exactly." She had no clue.

Dylan cocked her head and narrowed her eyes. "Let's tackle the simple question. I need to know if you're bringing a date to the premiere. If so, I'm not going to be the tagalong with you and Sam and your men. I'll need to find a date too."

"That's actually the complicated question. So, things have been wonderful. But now I'm not so sure." She rolled her shoulders back.

"Is that why you tip-toed in here at dawn?" Dylan's eyes widened.

Amanda frowned. So much for sneaking into the house. Stealthy, she was not. "Yeah. Jake got called for a fire at three a.m. and I couldn't get back to sleep. And it got me thinking."

"Thinking or overthinking? Is he okay?" Dylan arched a brow.

Amanda nodded. "I assume so. Right before you came in, the news was covering the fire and they said nobody was injured. But he hasn't texted me or anything yet."

"I thought you were just having a no-strings fling with the hot fireman. Did he tell you he'd text you? Is it getting serious?"

"Well, he took off in the middle of the night to a fire. I would think he'd let me know everything was fine. And it just…" She nibbled on her lower lip.

"It just worries you he might get called out and

never come home. Right?"

Amanda closed her eyes and exhaled a long breath. "For some reason, I just hadn't been thinking it through because, you know, the throw caution to the wind mentality. It might not be smart for someone like me to get involved with someone like him."

"Someone like you meaning you like a regular schedule or…?"

She shook her head. "No, someone like me who lost their mom and is terrified of letting anybody else close enough to be devastated if I lost them. I just don't know if I could handle opening up and letting him all the way in and lose him."

Dylan blew out a breath and leaned back in her chair. "Whoa. When you put it like that, I see your point. It is risky. For all of us."

Amanda thunked her head back against the chair. "Right? After he left, I flashed back to the grief from losing Mom. It felt like it was yesterday. I don't know if I can handle the not knowing if he's okay on a regular basis."

"Well, it's only been a few weeks with Jake. Can't you just date him and have fun for a while? I mean…hunky firefighter and all." Dylan fanned her hand in front of her face.

Amanda managed a slight smile. "I'm not like you. I wish I could just have fun and date around, but I'm not built that way. I thought I could have this fling, but it's feeling deeper already." *Like falling in love stage.*

Dylan's dark brows drew together. "Hey, I don't

always just flit around from guy to guy."

Amanda smiled for real this time. "I didn't mean it that way. But of all of us, you've dated the most and seem to always leave a trail of broken hearts behind you."

Dylan rolled her eyes. "Oh please. Trail of broken hearts? Hardly. I don't know. I just like guys and they like me. But, we've all focused on our careers and probably to the detriment of our love lives. I mean, if Holt hadn't rolled in here and swept Sam off her feet, we'd probably not even be having this discussion."

Amanda cocked her head. Dylan had a great point. Their tough, tomboy sister falling in love and the movie business had jolted them all out of their comfortable patterns. She'd always figured a guy would come along at just the right moment. Some point way off in the future. Jake was here now.

"You make it sound like we were all sleeping beauties in a fairy tale waiting to be kissed."

Dylan laughed. "Yes. Exactly that. The McNeill princesses. You and Sam, anyways. So back to my first question. The premiere is in a few weeks. I need to either get online or dig into my contacts to find a date if you're taking Jake. I think you should."

Amanda swallowed, her throat drying out. Could be the coffee, but more likely her nerves. "I need to think about it. How much time do you need to drum up a date? Two hours?"

"Very funny. At least three. Look, there's no

guy here who means anything to me. If Jake does, you should invite him." Dylan stood, her eyes twinkling.

"I'll figure it out in the next few days. Now are you going to tell me who texted you from France? Anything to do with last summer's soccer star?"

Dylan crossed the few feet separating them and leaned down for a hug. "Amanda, we're talking about you and Jake. I've never seen you look so relaxed and happy. Don't cut this short because you're scared to let him close. Give it a chance."

Amanda squeezed her younger sister. "We'll see." Although right now it made more sense to her to step away while they were still in the early stages of whatever it was they were doing together. Safer that way.

# CHAPTER 21

JAKE FROWNED AT HIS PHONE. Amanda's one word text looked ominous to him. After the emergency call, the shock of his dad's sentiments, and his eight-mile run, he'd collapsed on his bed. He'd slept for five hours straight. After he woke up, he'd texted Amanda to check on how she was doing. Her uncharacteristic reply didn't come for another few hours. Strange.

But she could've been working or at physical therapy or doing a million other things than sitting by her phone waiting for him to contact her. He massaged the tightness at the back of his neck and considered how to respond to her one-word text.

*Busy.*

That was it. Nothing referring to last night or referring to seeing him again. No questions about the middle of the night emergency call. Nothing inviting a discussion. Hell, maybe she was simply in the middle of work.

*Sorry about last night. Can I make it up to you over dinner? Pick you up at 7?*

When she didn't respond within fifteen minutes, Jake paced around his apartment. He checked the dark screen one more time and his shoulders sagged. He looked around his apartment and exhaled a frustrated breath. Okay, if she was blowing him off, he needed to do something productive. He couldn't go running again so maybe he'd hit the gym, throw around some weights. But for once, working out didn't appeal.

The computer drew his gaze and he stared at it and the pile of textbooks stacked on his desk. "Damn it." He stomped over to the desk, yanked out the chair, and sat.

He dropped his head into his hands. The problem was his dad had thrown a wrench into what seemed like a clear plan. His career was incredible. He loved being an integral part of his community and helping people. Although he loved his job as a fire engineer, he'd convinced himself the path to fire captain was the only correct one. But maybe for some of the wrong reasons.

No matter how surprising and affirming it had been to hear his dad utter the words he'd waited for his whole lifetime, he wanted more for himself. He did want to be captain. He did want to inspire and lead a team. He knew he'd be excellent at it and he wanted to do it. He'd get his degree, even if it took him a long time. He'd do it for himself. Nobody else.

His phone pinged and he surged out of the chair and grabbed it. *Are you free in an hour or so? We need to talk.*

Jake squeezed his eyes shut and stalked around

the room again. It was worse than he'd anticipated: Amanda didn't want to go to dinner and she'd raised the four words every man alive dreaded: We. Need. To. Talk.

What had happened from their perfect night until now? Well, besides his three a.m. work call? He crossed the room to the couch, sank down, and dropped his head back against the soft cushions. Part of him wanted to pretend he hadn't seen her message. Wait until tomorrow to deal with it.

Yeah, right. Like he would be able to sleep. Come to think of it, he probably wasn't going to sleep after his long-ass nap. No one could accuse him of being a chicken, but nothing had scared him like falling head over heels for Amanda.

His job was a true reason not to get too intimate with any woman, but if he were honest with himself, he did compare every woman he'd dated to Amanda. And now the daydreams had become a dream come true.

For a few short weeks. Despite his brain urging him to be careful because logic dictated he'd be consumed with loving Amanda McNeill, his heart did back flips whenever she was on his mind. If he relinquished these tutoring boundaries he'd erected between them, would he be able to hold back sharing his deepening feelings with her?

Better find out now. He grabbed his phone. *Sure. Where?*

*Why don't I meet you at the beach with Stella?*

Not really what he'd hoped for, but he'd take Amanda any way he could. *Del Mar Dog Beach?*

*She can go off leash.*

*I'll meet you at 5.* The screen went black.

It was rare anybody sent shorter texts or had terser replies than he did, but apparently Amanda could be succinct. He sighed.

He hopped in the shower. Good news was the sun set around 5:45 p.m., setting up the opportunity for a romantic sunset. Maybe he was being paranoid and they would take Stella for a walk, discuss whatever was on her mind, and everything would be great. Maybe even end up having dinner too.

He would use everything in his power to convince her exploring their relationship was the right choice.

Amanda rubbed her hands over her face and squeezed her eyes closed. When she opened them, the beauty of the California coastline hit her senses. The kiss of the crisp salty breeze and the hint of warmth from the late afternoon sun should have improved her mood. Even the power of a watercolor azure and white sky couldn't alleviate the heaviness weighing down her limbs and the melancholy in her heart. Not even the dozen or so dogs frolicking in the foaming surf made her smile. Not even Stella's grinning face and joyous zeal playing fetch helped.

Not when she couldn't envision how she could handle Jake's career for the long-term. Up until last night, their budding relationship was primarily light and fun. Already, they'd been zooming along at a breakneck pace from the moment he'd shown up like a Good Samaritan with Stella bleeding in his arms.

Their prior connection, their current bargain, and their undeniable physical chemistry were incredible. Heck, he'd shown up at a crossroads in her life where she was questioning everything she'd always accepted as fact. Shown up looking all heroic and beautiful and strong and vulnerable at the same time. What woman could resist a man like him?

Maybe if she were a different person, she could enjoy the present moment and not fret over the future. But she wasn't built for amusement park rides that thrilled for the short-term and abruptly ended. Being in his arms touched her deeper, all the way into her heart. She was built for the long and slow and falling in love with a firefighter didn't fit slow and steady.

How could she survive it? The waiting and wondering if he were okay triggered her. Everything she thought about herself: practical, calm, steady, in control? Out the window. Her nervous system and her deeply buried trauma from losing her mom burst to the surface, exploding into the present moment. She couldn't risk that type of devastation again. Couldn't lose someone she loved decades too soon.

One night of an emergency call and she was completely undone.

Unraveled.

Jake was an amazing man, but his chosen career was fraught with danger. Although she couldn't control when someone might be taken from her, she was analytical enough to know how to minimize risk. And she would to protect herself. Her head needed to continue ruling her heart.

No matter how much she wanted him to be the one. No matter how much she wanted him to be her partner for life. No matter how intensely deep her feelings were in such a short period of time. She had to discover where he stood. Would he ever consider a different role in the fire department? How could she even ask it of him?

And didn't that throw a dark shadowy veil over the Del Mar scenery tonight? Amanda's fingers curled into her palms and she struggled to regulate her breath.

She sensed his presence before he spoke. She turned toward him. Tried not to allow the square line of his jaw or the curve of his gentle smile to sway her resolve.

"Hi." He smiled at Amanda and shifted his gaze to the animal loping toward them. "There's my girl." Stella galloped up and yipped and danced around him, like she hadn't just seen him hours ago. He crouched down and hugged the dog close, despite her wet sandy fur.

Amanda's heart clenched at his words. *My girl.* Lucky girl was more like it. What if her questions resulted in separating him from the dog he'd rescued? If worse came to worse, she'd figure out some way for him to keep her on a part-time basis. Hopefully, it wouldn't reach that point.

"Want to walk her up toward the cliffs and throw the ball for her?" Amanda gestured to the sandstone carved cliffs framing the north end of dog beach. Fewer people and dogs were close to the rocks, so they'd have greater opportunity for a private conversation.

Jake nodded and pressed up to his full height. She swallowed, her throat parched, her rehearsed words evaporating and floating away like gossamer in the wind. She started walking toward the cliffs, keeping her gaze forward and avoiding the temptation of succumbing to his sheer masculine presence. *Do not look at him. Do not touch him. Focus on what needs to happen.*

They strolled in silence, Stella trotting ahead of them, intermittently angling her head back, as if to encourage them to hurry up already.

"I saw you on the news." Her voice came out in a whisper.

His head whipped toward her. "What? I saw the cameras, but didn't think they filmed me."

She swallowed again. "Well, not you exactly. But I saw the news when I got home this morning. And I assumed you were one of the guys in the background after you'd been called in."

"Yeah, luckily it was handled quickly."

They paused at the edge of the foaming surf. When he remained silent, she gathered her resolve. Stella ran back and spit a grimy tennis ball at their feet. Jake picked it up and tossed it out into the surf and Stella ran back into the pounding waves to retrieve it.

Amanda turned to look at him. "So, we need to talk."

"That's what you said on the phone." His tone gave nothing away.

"Look Jake, I'm not good at this kind of thing…" She swallowed again, her heartbeat thundering in her temples.

"This type of thing?" His black brows arched above the rim of his mirrored aviators.

"Things happened really fast between us. With Stella and…well, this." She waved one hand between the two of them.

"This?"

Damn him for his monosyllabic replies. "This. Whatever it is we've been doing these last few weeks."

"You need to spell it out for me." He spoke through stiff lips, his jaw now carved from granite harder than the cliffs behind him.

She blew out a breath. "Well, this is awkward. I'm just not sure what we're doing. I mean, are we just friends with benefits or is it something more?"

He shrugged. "What do you want it to be?"

Amanda's gut clenched, then Stella provided a moment of comic relief when she ran up and shook half the ocean all over them, then spat the ball at their feet. Jake repeated his earlier action and tossed the ball even further out. Stella sped away.

He wasn't going to make this easy. "Okay, well

it all seemed simple at first, but at this point in my life——"

"At this point in your life what?" He stared out at the ocean, his profile unyielding.

She huffed out a breath and threaded her icy fingers together. None of the words were coming out the way they'd sounded when she'd rehearsed the speech in her mind. "I think we need to define whatever it is we've been doing. You're a great guy, but I don't..."

The coldness in her fingers began to creep up and fill her being, moving steadily toward her heart.

"Was it last night's fire call?" His jaw was tight.

She nodded. "That's part of it. It just made me realize we'd jumped into this too fast and that's not how I work."

"Weren't you the one who kissed me first?" Now his tone was remote.

Heat flooded her cheeks. She wasn't frozen after all. "Yes, but..." What could she say?

"So you can just turn it on and off?" His voice was quiet.

She turned to look at him again. "Of course not. I just realized——"

"Realized you shouldn't get involved with someone not in your life plan, whatever that is?" How could his voice sound so unemotional?

"Jake, I don't have a life plan. I just think we moved too fast. Your job scares me and I hadn't thought that through." *Please tell me I'm overreacting or something.* She dug her fingernails into her icy palms.

"What, you want me to quit my job? Seriously?" He whipped off his sunglasses and his eyes were two obsidian chips.

"No. Yes. I don't know. Can we discuss it?" She pressed her lips together to stop them from trembling.

"Discuss it? You know my career is my whole life. All I've ever wanted to do. It's who I am."

Amanda shifted her hands up to rub her arms. "I didn't say I wanted you to quit your job. I just want––"

"If you're scared of what I do, we've got a problem. What about Stella?"

She squeezed her arms, seeking some respite from the numbness. "You rescued her and I know you can't keep her full time. We can keep sharing her––we'll figure it out."

"Won't that interrupt your life plan?" His tone was frigid.

To her horror, tears rose behind her eyes and her throat felt raw. "Of course not. We can share her and be friends. It's not a big deal."

He blew out a breath again. "Friends. Great. Fine. Is that all?"

"Jake?"

"I've got things to do so, if that's it, I'm going to head out. Text me what time to pick up Stella." He pivoted away from her.

"I––" Why couldn't she string together a full sentence? Why did her heart feel frozen in her chest?

"It would be great if you weren't around when I pick her up." Jake stared out at the water and whistled for the dog.

Stella returned with the ball, but her tail hung limply between her legs, her chocolate gaze shifting between the two of them. Jake scratched her ears. "See you soon, sweet girl." He turned and marched off down the beach.

Amanda remained rooted to the packed sand beneath her feet and watched him disappear. Her legs shook and the tears that had been threatening fulfilled their promise and poured down her cheeks in hot torrents. She sank down to her knees and buried her face in her hands.

Stella whimpered and rubbed against her. Amanda wrapped an arm around the dog's soaking wet torso and sobbed. What had she done?

# CHAPTER 22

JAKE PULLED UP TO THE McNeill estate, parked the car, and forced himself to cross the ground to the front door. Because he'd volunteered to cover extra shifts, he hadn't been up to the house in a week. His four day break started today and fortunately, Amanda had agreed Stella could stay with him the whole time. He needed the comfort of time with the pup. He'd filled his days with work, studying, and punishing workouts designed to exhaust him to his limits so he could fall into bed and escape into a dreamless slumber. No way was he ready to see Amanda again after she'd basically broken things off. They hadn't spoken in the week since the awful evening at the beach.

Everything in his apartment reminded him of her. The couch. The bed. The frickin' kitchen counter. It was pathetic. Just like him. How could she even consider asking him to give up his career? She knew he'd dreamt of being a firefighter since he was kid. Knew how much he wanted to become fire captain. Knew how his career had never seemed enough for his dad and now it wasn't enough for her either. Hell, she'd been the one encouraging him to follow his dreams.

Despite agreeing her fears were justified about losing him in a fire, he wanted her anyway. Wanted her by his side as his life partner. Wanted her in his bed when he came home, whether from a routine shift at the station or from whatever blazing hellish inferno he had to battle. Other firefighters were married and had families. If two people wanted to make it work, they would.

But she had a "life plan" that didn't include him. Apparently, her current plan had been simple––have a fun fling with him. The physical chemistry was undeniable, but as she'd said, not part of her life "plan." Nothing serious or permanent. She'd admitted she'd been in a rut and was looking to change things up. Maybe that's all he was and when life became more serious with his work call, she ran.

He could have tried to convince her. Tried to fight for her. But who was he kidding? He *agreed* with her. She was right. She deserved a man who went to work every day and slept at home every night. A man she wouldn't fear losing every time he went to work. How could she ever separate the loss of her mom when she was still a teenager from the fear of loving someone with a career like his?

He raked his hands through his hair and tugged. Maybe the pain could counteract the truth surrounding her concerns? He wasn't wired for anything else. Had never wanted anything else but what he was doing. He couldn't work in an office. Or sell things. He was wired to protect. Wired to defend. Wired to do exactly what he was doing.

And Amanda McNeill didn't want the risk. Didn't want him enough to try. Had he really been kidding himself that she'd fall in love with him? That they'd be a couple?

He'd spent his whole life trying to convince his dad he was good enough. He wouldn't spend the rest of his life trying to convince Amanda he was worthy.

He'd spend the rest of his life or as long as the fire department would have him, handling emergencies. He'd get his degree and become captain and help other firefighters achieve their dreams of making a difference. And maybe somewhere along that timeline, a woman would show up who did find him to be enough without trying to change him. Who understood the risks of his career and wanted him despite them. Or even because of them.

Amanda McNeill had always been the dream. One he'd never imagined would become a reality, even for a short while. Dreams were fleeting. He'd hold this one close and then bury it down deep. Just another layer of his experience. Another period of time in his life that had ended.

He trudged toward the enormous wooden front door, the gravel crunching beneath his running shoes. If his heart was racing like it had been during his run earlier this morning, so be it.

Before he could knock on the door, it opened. Dylan stood in the doorway, Stella by her side. "Hi, Jake." Her smile was warm, and reached her dark eyes.

"Hey, Dylan." He returned her smile and gazed down at the dog. "Hey, girl, ready to go to the beach?"

Stella wagged her tail and pressed against his legs.

"She's happy to see you and I'm sure she'll love the beach. Poor thing has been stuck out at the ranch all week."

He laughed. "Yeah, tough life she's got here." Part of him was relieved to see Dylan instead of Amanda, but the rest of him ached. Damn, he missed her.

Dylan pulled the door closed behind her. "Can I walk you to your truck?"

"Escorting me off the property?" He tried for a joke, but it fell flat.

She patted his arm. "Don't be silly. Look, you and I don't know each other, but I know my sister. And she's unhappy. She won't talk about it, but I'm figuring since she asked me to bring Stella out and she's silent and miserable, something happened."

Jake rubbed the tight cords on the back of his neck. No reason to avoid the truth. "Basically she made it clear things wouldn't work out with us."

Dylan frowned. "Did she say why?"

"Shouldn't you ask her?"

"Well, if you understand my sister even a little bit, she's the master at acting like everything is fine. Even when it is obviously not fine. She's eating even less than usual, she hasn't laughed in a week, and she won't tell Sam or me what's going on. Please?"

He sighed. "She said she didn't think she could handle my career. Said seeing me didn't fit with her plan. That's it."

Dylan sighed. "I figured it had to be something like that. Was this after that fire that was on TV?"

He nodded.

Her dark brows drew together and she squeezed his arm. "Did she explain to you how we lost our mom? What that did to our family?"

"Yeah. I'm sorry, by the way." The McNeills had endured hell.

She waved away his apology. "Look, it changed our lives completely. But, it's been over twelve years now. I've never seen her as happy as she has been since you two started hanging out. And now I haven't seen her so unhappy since right after our mom passed."

"I'm sorry. But she was pretty clear." His job wouldn't work for her.

"Well, did you try to convince her otherwise?" She narrowed her eyes.

"Convince her of what? That I won't die? My job is dangerous. It's all I've ever wanted and all I'll ever do. I can't change that." And couldn't be with someone who would ask for that sacrifice.

Dylan chewed on the inside of her cheek. "I think she's really into you. I think you two could be great together. I think you should talk to her. Give it some more time."

"Look, I appreciate what you're saying, but your sister deserves a guy who is educated and stable and secure, not someone like me." Someone like his damn brother, Rafe.

Dylan huffed. "No, she does not. You just described her exactly. She doesn't need to date herself. Someone like you is exactly what she needs."

"You don't know me. I'm not the guy for her." He shook his head.

"Do you want to be?" Her voice grew serious.

He closed his eyes and rubbed his jaw. "I had a crush on her from the time I was in ninth grade. She's a dream come true. But I'm not enough for her and I'm not giving up my career or trying to convince her of it. Okay?"

"What? Why would you think you're not enough? She thinks you're incredible. She's just frightened. She needs someone like you to pull her out of her comfort zone. Someone to make her feel taken care of. Reassured."

He shook his head, but something in his chest was shifting. Did she really think he was incredible? Had she really just been looking for reassurance from him because she was afraid?

"Look. All I know is you made her happier than I've seen her since we were kids. That doesn't come along very often, sometimes never." Her dark brows drew together. "I think you should fight for her."

He spread his hands out. "Even if you're right, I wouldn't even know what to do. She doesn't want to talk to me or see me. Nothing besides text about the dog."

"Because she's scared and stubborn." Her full lips, so like her older sisters', hitched up. "I have an idea."

"What?" His heartbeat accelerated.

"We've got to go to the premiere of the movie my dad helped direct last summer on the ranch. None of my sisters or I have been back to L.A. since we left. We've agreed to go, but we're all dreading it, to be honest. My dad thinks it will help with closure." She shrugged.

"That makes sense. Maybe the idea of Hollywood won't seem so big anymore." He cocked his head. "But I don't get what this has to do with me."

"Amanda's dreading this. What if you came?"

"Huh?"

"What if I get you a ticket to the premiere and you come and walk the red carpet with her. Show her you can be there when it matters. To back her up. My sister has always been the caretaker. Show her she doesn't have to always be so strong." Dylan was nodding now.

He shook his head. "I don't know. I don't know how me going to a movie would—"

Dylan plowed on like he hadn't spoken. "Yes, this is the perfect plan. The paparazzi harassed us like something out of a bad reality show. None of us want to walk the red carpet and deal with reporters. You could be the buffer for her."

"They'd probably think I'm a bodyguard." He frowned.

"No, you could be the hero. Her hero. She knows as well as the rest of us that life is short and uncertain. You guys have a chance to have something really special. She just needs to believe you're really there for her. That you are crazy about her. You love her, right?" Dylan demanded.

His chest tightened. Hell yes he loved her. "How are you so sure she's in love with me?"

"Because I've known her my whole life. You two are perfect together. Are you in?"

Jake held his breath for a moment. Could he really open himself up like this? To get his heart ripped out? Hell yes. Amanda was worth every risk in the world.

Adrenaline coursed through his veins. "Well, what do you want me to do? Ask her or..."

"Let me take care of it. I'll text you with the date and time and where to meet us. You okay driving up to L.A.?" Dylan flashed her white teeth.

"As long as I'm not on shift, yeah."

"Can you get coverage if you are? Swap with someone or something?"

Tenacity had to be a McNeill trait. "Probably. Look, this all sounds a little over the top...I'm not sure——"

"What do you have to lose? You've got every-thing to gain."

She was right. He'd already lost her. His pride and his heart were already battered. He'd fought for everything that mattered in his life. "I'll do it."

# CHAPTER 23

AMANDA DRAINED THE LAST DROPS of champagne and set the crystal flute into the fancy stretch limousine's drink holder. Her nerves thrummed and disquiet filled her. When their father had convinced them to attend the movie premiere, she'd assumed they'd make a discreet entrance and exit. Forcing them to walk the red carpet seemed unreasonable and unnecessary.

The last time they'd gone to one of her parent's premieres, the whole family had walked together. Her mom had been nominated for an Oscar and a Golden Globe for best actress. Amanda had only been thirteen years old, on the cusp between child and young woman, and she'd been thrilled to participate in all the glitz and glamour. She could still picture the bright lights sparkling off her little sisters' matching caramel-colored gowns. They'd all been so innocent.

What a contrast tonight. All the memories she'd locked away where she'd loved having parents in the entertainment industry rose to the surface. How she and her sisters had loved the famous people her parents socialized with, the movies and television shows they were lucky enough to see early, and the parties her parents would throw. How exciting it all used to appear.

Before the accident, reporters calling her mom and dad's names had filled her with pride: her parents were a talented, respected power couple and Amanda had loved seeing them bask in the spotlight.

How quickly it had turned ugly after the accident. She shook herself back to the present. The past was the past.

Tonight would be fine. She glanced across the limo, where Sam was cuddled into Holt's side, exuding contentment. For years, her sister had kept men at arm's length and focused on being the best in her industry. Now she was not only one of the most respected horse breeders in the country, she was madly in love with a man who worshiped the ground she walked on.

Her dad was bouncing on his seat like a little boy about to get his first puppy. A smiling Angela held his hand. A decade in and Angela's warmth and strength continued to be the glue keeping their family together.

Amanda sighed. Her dad had not only lost his wife, but also given up his successful career to give his daughters a chance at a life away from the harassment of paparazzi and fickleness of the movie industry. He deserved this renaissance of his directing career.

Dylan looked stunning as usual, her auburn hair cascading around her shoulders, her creamy oval face glowing in the dim light as she sipped her champagne. Like she didn't have a care in the world.

Was she overreacting? If everyone else seemed fine with attending the premiere, shouldn't she?

But the real issue, besides being about to walk the red carpet wearing emerald silk, was she missed Jake. Not seeing him these past few weeks and going the cowardly route of having Dylan bring Stella out to him had been tough, but she couldn't sleep. Couldn't eat. How had she fallen for him so fast? From the moment he appeared on her doorstep with Stella, everything had changed. Had she made a mistake trying to push him for answers so soon? Maybe she should have just gone with the flow like Dylan suggested. Seen what happened and maybe figured out ways to manage her fears?

Every time she looked at the dog, she pictured Jake's strong hands ruffling her fur.

When she tried to go to the beach again with Stella, she'd turned around before reaching her car and taken the dog for a walk along the fields of the ranch instead. The beach reminded her of Jake. Of meeting his family. Of their sexy hike at Torrey Pines. Of how he'd encouraged her to do something different. To get out of her rut and try something new with him.

Most of all, it reminded her she'd handled their last discussion poorly. She'd hoped for reassurance or suggestions of what she could do when he was out on calls to manage her stress. She'd wanted to explain how isolated and alone she'd felt with how she'd learned of her mom's death. But nothing had come out how she'd planned and Jake's reaction, while not surprising, had been devastating.

Her stomach tightened. Yes, she was being contrary. But she'd really wanted him to talk it through with her. All she'd wanted was for him to comfort her after she'd witnessed him take off at three a.m. Of course she'd never ask him to give up his career, but she'd wanted some acknowledgment of her fears. That's all. But she'd bungled it.

He'd just nodded and walked away. If it weren't for the dog, she'd probably never hear from him again. Her shoulders slumped back against the cool buttery leather seat. She wasn't the type of woman people fought for because she was too good at pretending she didn't need anything. He'd assumed she didn't care.

"Amanda, come on. We're here. You ready?" Dylan asked. Her family was staring at her like she'd sprouted a unicorn horn.

"Sorry. Of course." Why did she have to be sitting closest to the door and be the first one out? Oh yeah, because she always took charge. Was always fine. She squared her shoulders and prepared to face Los Angeles.

The chauffer opened the door and the noise was deafening. They were at the curb, right at the start of the red carpet at the Grauman's Chinese Theatre. Flash bulbs blinded her, the close Los Angeles air flooded her lungs, and for a moment she froze.

"Go on Amanda, we can't hold up the line." Sam called from the depths of the limousine.

Unable to see because of the flashing lights, Amanda accepted the chauffer's large hand and with an unsteady breath, stepped out of the limo. She stood and stepped to the side to allow her family to join her. Suddenly, she realized the chauffer still gripped her hand. What the heck?

She pulled her hand free and looked up to see what the guy's deal was. Her jaw fell open when a broad chest, covered in a dark navy suit, met her eyes. She lifted her gaze up to his face and her eyes widened. "Jake?"

He flashed a sexy grin at her. "At your service."

"What in the world are you doing here?" The heat from his proximity was warming her skin. Her brain blanked and her heartbeat accelerated, knocking against her ribs.

"I'm here to walk you down the red carpet." He reached for her hand again and wound his fingers through hers.

"I——" How had he known? Why was he here? Why would he do this?

Her dad's voice came from beside her. "It's time. You girls follow behind Angela and me. No stopping, just smile if you can, okay?" Her dad smiled at her and nodded at Jake.

When had the rest of her family exited the limo? Before she could question what he was doing there, Amanda found herself gliding down the red carpet, her hand grasped firmly against Jake's warm, dry skin. The cacophony of noise faded and the lights seemed to disappear in the distance. All she could feel was Jake.

"There's Jack and Ella!" Amanda dimly heard the screams when the stars of the movie stepped from the next limo.

Nobody yelled her name. Nobody screamed questions about her mom. Nobody really seemed to notice them. They reached the cool interior of the theater and joined her waiting family. Jake beside her every step of the way.

"See? Nobody even noticed us. All they care about is the stars. Harry's already inside. Is everyone okay?" Her dad looked around, and then nodded to Jake. "Nice to see you, Jake."

Sam and Dylan answered together. "You were right. Not a big deal."

"Hey, they could've at least asked me some questions, I mean hey, I did all the scary stunts." Holt protested.

"We'll buy you a drink, Holt." Chris laughed. "You've all got your tickets, so just meet at the seats before it starts." Her family left her alone with Jake.

Dylan turned and winked at Amanda, following everyone else to the bar.

Before she could move, Jake turned her to face him and rested his hands on her shoulders. "Dylan invited me."

Amanda's heart was pounding. "Why did you come?"

Jake inhaled deeply and blew out his breath. "I've missed you, Amanda. I'm crazy about you and I think you were wrong."

Amanda drew back. "I was wrong?"

He nodded. "I know you're scared and I know my career is dangerous. But you and I have something special. Something that doesn't come along often. Will you give me a chance to make you happy?"

She bit her lip, but warmth was spreading through her limbs and her spine was tingling. "What are you saying?"

"I'm saying I love you. I want us to take our time and go slow and steady or whatever pace works for you. Despite the risks. Despite knowing I don't deserve someone like you. I want to be the person you can rely on to always be there for you, even though you're the strongest person I know."

Her heart burst with joy. "Love?"

He frowned. "Do you think you could love me?"

She threw her arms around him. "I do love you. That's why I was asking you to tell me everything would be okay at the beach. I'm sorry it all came out wrong."

He pulled her in tight to his rock-hard body. "That's not what it sounded like."

She melted against him. "If I didn't care about you, I wouldn't care about losing you. I was scared."

"You don't have to be afraid. I'm here. I can't guarantee what will happen, but there aren't any guarantees in life. I love you and will spend the rest of my life doing everything in my power to be the best partner."

"Yes." She pulled his face down to meet hers and kissed him hard.

Applause erupted around them. They drew apart and looked around. Her family had gathered and in the front, Dylan stood with two flutes of champagne.

"Now that's a great Hollywood ending."

She looked into Jake's eyes and laughed. "I'd say so."

# EPILOGUE

*Three months later*

AMANDA SMOOTHED AN ERRANT STRAND of hair away from her face. A warm summer breeze caressed her cheeks and kept the temperature reasonable, but wasn't really working out with her sleek blow-dried hair. She should have worn it back in her customary ponytail, but today was special and she'd wanted to feel special too. The flutter in her belly kicked up to a flapping of wings when Jake pulled up and parked his truck. She exhaled an unsteady breath and strolled to meet him.

A broad grin flashed across Jake's bronzed face and his powerful arms pulled her into his solid torso. With a growl low in his throat, he captured her mouth in a hot kiss. She slid her arms up his broad chest and laced her fingers behind his strong neck. A shiver danced down her spine.

He tipped his head back and smiled down at her. "Hi beautiful. How was volunteering with the rescue group today and where's Stella?"

Once her shoulder had healed, Amanda had

been volunteering a few times a month. "It was great, but she's mad at me when she smelled all the other dogs on me and is off pouting."

Jake laughed. "She definitely doesn't like you cheating on her."

Amanda grinned. "Right? No, she's down at the guesthouse. I figured we could go over and get her for our walk."

He fell into step beside her and they headed hand-in-hand across the verdant lawn. Amanda focused on regulating her breathing and enjoying the firm grip of his fingers intertwined with hers. Grateful for their ability to spend time together without filling the space with chatter, she savored the firmness of the earth beneath her feet and the warmth of the sun's rays on her skin.

Jake stopped in front of the first guesthouse, where Sam and Holt lived. Amanda tugged his hand. "Come on, we're not stopping here."

One dark eyebrow arched. "I thought you said Stella was in the guesthouse?"

She shook her head and her lips hitched up. "Not this guesthouse. Follow me." She tugged his hand again.

"I don't get it? Why is she in one of the other guesthouses?" Despite his questions, he accompanied her farther away from the main house, toward where two smaller single-story homes were located.

Amanda quickened her steps along the palm-tree-shrouded path before she lost her nerve. She couldn't explain to him yet——she needed to be inside the second guesthouse. Her pulse began to thrum.

"Here we go." She paused in front of the Spanish-style cottage with its cream-colored walls and terracotta roof, released his hand, and opened the teal blue front door.

Stella bounded toward them across the warm honey-colored hardwood floors and skidded to a stop at their feet. Skylights on the high tongue-and-groove ceiling bathed the wide foyer with natural light and a sense of openness.

"It's kind of big for a dog house, don't you think?" Jake laughed and bent down to scratch the enthusiastic mutt's ears.

Amanda cleared her throat. "It's not too big for you, me, and Stella though, is it?" She blew out an enormous exhale and raised her gaze to his.

"What?" He froze and his gorgeous brown eyes widened.

"Well, I've been thinking we spend so much time together now and maybe it would make sense if we lived under the same roof. The cottage has four bedrooms, so there's room for an office and a guest room and…" Amanda's heart was galloping in her chest.

Jake was beaming at her. "Wait, are you asking me to live with you? For us to live together here at the ranch?"

"Yes, I mean, unless you didn't want to live with me or live on the ranch?" Although now he was laughing at her like her proposition was the funniest thing he'd ever heard.

"Why are you laughing at me?" *What the heck?*

Jake crossed the few steps separating them and clasped both of her hands in his. "I'm not laughing at you. I'm laughing at us. I think we're on the same page."

"You do?" *Say yes already!*

Keeping ahold of her hands, Jake dropped to one knee and looked up at her. "Maybe I'm a little ahead of you. I was planning on taking you down to the beach later to ask you, but now seems better."

"Ask me?" Buzzing began in her ears and tingling began at the crown of her head and traveled down to her feet.

"Amanda, you were my first love. My only love. You are the kindest person I know and showed me how much power there is in being patient. You are the smartest person I've ever met, but you helped me feel confident about school. You're the most beautiful woman I've ever seen, not just on the outside, but in your heart, where it counts. I don't know what I did to get so lucky, but now that we're together I don't want to let you go. Ever." He swallowed, but kept his dark gaze locked with hers.

"Jake, I…"

"Now I know my high school crush can't compare to loving you. Amanda, will you marry me?"

Her hands were shaking, her heart was racing, and joy filled her heart. "Jake Cruz, you are the perfect man for me. I would be honored to be your wife. Yes, absolutely yes."

Jake kept one of her hands clasped in his and pulled out a blue velvet box with the other, flicking it open. "When I saw this ring, it reminded me of your beautiful green eyes. More warm than a diamond." He slid the princess cut emerald on a delicate pave diamond band onto her finger.

Amanda gasped and pulled Jake to his feet and threw herself into his arms. "I love it. I absolutely love that you would know I'd prefer something unique like this."

He picked her up and swung her around in a circle. Stella barked and danced around their feet, eager to join in the celebration. Amanda's heartbeat slowed and a sense of peace filled her despite the twirling around.

She gazed down at the sweet dog who'd been the catalyst for bringing Jake back into her life, then lifted her gaze to his. "You still haven't answered my question."

"Yes, I would love to live here with you and Stella. Does that mean she's officially ours?" He smiled down at the dog.

Amanda nodded and slid her hands into his dense, silky hair and wrapped her legs around his waist. "She'll be okay for a little while. There's a room I wanted to show you."

Jake's eyes grew hooded. "Oh really?"

"If you'll just carry me down the hall here to the left, I'll show you. I want to make sure you approve of the master bedroom." She pulled his head down the few inches to meet her kiss.

He strode down the hallway, holding her tight, with his mouth fused to hers. "Yes. Definitely yes."

## THE END

# OTHER BOOKS BY

*Second Chance in Laguna*
*At Last in Laguna*
*Sunset in Laguna*
*Nobody Else But You*

Thank you for reading *The Very Thought of You*! I hope you loved Amanda and Jake's sweet story. The next book in the Pacific Vista Ranch series is *For The Love of You* and is a fake engagement love story featuring Dylan McNeill and French soccer star Gabriel DuVernay. Coming early 2020. *www. clairemarti.com/mybooks.html*

To find out about new books, book signings and events, and receive exclusive giveaways and sneak peeks of future books, sign up for my newsletter: *www.clairemarti.com*

If you love steamy beach romances, check out my award winning Finding Forever in Laguna series. You'll find previews of *Second Chance in Laguna, At Last in Laguna*, and *Sunset in Laguna* here: *www. clairemarti.com/mybooks.html*

And if you have a moment, please leave a review for *The Very Thought of You* on your favorite book site.

# AUTHOR BIO

CLAIRE MARTI STARTED WRITING STORIES as soon as she was old enough to pick up pencil and paper. After graduating from the University of Virginia with a BA in English Literature, Claire was sidetracked by other careers, including practicing law, selling software for legal publishers, and managing a non-profit animal rescue for a Hollywood actress.

Finally, Claire followed her heart and now focuses on two of her true passions: writing romance and teaching yoga. She lives in San Diego with her husband and furry kids.